WEEKEND  WiFE

WEEKEND WIFE

NEW YORK TIMES BESTSELLING AUTHOR

ERIN McCARTHY

Interior Design and Formatting by

www.emtippettsbookdesigns.com

CHAPTER 1

My grandmother always said the way to a man's heart is through his stomach. With the man on the other side of the diner counter from me it might be easier to go through the fourth and fifth ribs.

Every Wednesday Grant Caldwell the third ordered chocolate chip pancakes with extra butter and real maple syrup and ate them like he was being force-fed sand dollars. Never a smile, never any joy.

"Why doesn't he look at his phone while he's eating like every other normal person?" Theresa muttered to me as she bustled past to grab the coffee pot. She bumped my hip on purpose when I didn't give an actual answer to her rhetorical question.

I had been too busy staring at the sheer masculine perfection of him. His dark short hair, bright blue eyes, and strong jaw were enough to tempt the average woman. Add in a tidy beard, *very* broad shoulders in an impeccable suit, and a red power tie, and I was fighting the constant urge to grab that tie by the knot and kiss the bejeesuz out of him.

For six months he'd been sitting there looking hot, and for six months my curiosity (and very naughty crush) had been growing. I didn't want a way into his heart so much as I wanted a way into his bed.

I gave Theresa a warning look. She wasn't exactly a woman with a soft voice. He was going to hear her.

But she was right. He never swiped on his phone or read a book or played with his napkin. He was always still and ate with singular determination, while ignoring my super obvious and very juvenile attempts to flirt with him. I'm an actress (you can't *quite* call it paid, but I'm working on it) so I'm not subtle. I'm frankly over-the-top. I know this about me and I embrace it.

I had tried food innuendos.

What else can I get you? Wink, wink.

You don't mind getting sticky, do you?

I see you have quite an appetite.

He never flirted back, sticking to noncommittal replies.

There was nothing from him when I sang either. That was the schtick in the diner. Aspiring and part-time actors waiting tables while struggling to break into a Broadway (or any) show. We sang, sometimes at the diners' request, other times just to liven up a quiet shift and hopefully beef up our tips. I had positioned myself in front of him on several Wednesdays singing my heart out from upbeat Disney songs to Les Miserable to a modern interpretation of "Hello" by Lionel Richie. I mean, Lionel Richie, people. *Hello*. That should have been worth a raised eyebrow or two but he just sat and ate and looked so damn beautiful that it hurt.

I wanted him like peanut butter wants jelly. Smashed together until there was no pulling us apart.

Yep. He was that hot.

And I was dressed like prude Sandy in Grease—ponytail, poodle skirt, bobby socks and all. It's a uniform, not a fashion choice. In my off-hours, I lean toward Slutty Sandy, minus the cigarette.

"I think he meditates," I told her under my breath, turning my back to him so he couldn't hear me.

"I think he's a cyborg. He has no response to normal stimuli."

That made me laugh. I grabbed my latest order and hoisted my tray. "Watch this."

In six months I had learned there was only one way to get Grant Caldwell to actually smile. Having creeped on his platinum credit card on day one or maybe two I had made note of his pretentious name. It seemed super fitting for him. He wore that name as well as his suit. It also sparked an instant correlation in my mind.

I sailed past him with my tray and cheerfully called out, "Hi, Grant!"

He tried not to smile but I could see the corner of his mouth tugging upward against his will. He shook his head a little. "Hi, Leah."

Yes, I had creeped on his credit card, but months ago he'd also creeped on my name badge. Normal, right? But it still gave me a thrill that he'd made note of my name. Which, you know, is right in his sightline. It wasn't like he'd gone out of his way. *But* he used it. It felt like a victory of epic proportions for a man who appeared to have zero emotions.

I'm an optimist. I had to be, given the amount of audition rejections I'd gotten. So Grant using my name was all I needed to think that given another six months, we might actually have a conversation. In about five years maybe we would graduate to sex, which was honestly the goal. Have I mentioned he was hot?

The first two times I'd called out "Hi, Grant!" for no apparent reason, he had been puzzled. Theresa had been dying laughing. But once I'd explained to him that I was channeling Goldie Hawn in Overboard and that it was the greatest rom-com ever, he'd appeared curious.

I'd bet a whole weeks' worth of tips he'd gone home to what I assumed was an expensive and masculine apartment with sleek electronics and had watched the movie.

Because the next week he'd smiled.

And then I couldn't stop myself from repeating it every week.

Because when he smiled, he went from damn good looking to holy shit hot.

He was a challenge. A nut to crack.

I was nothing if not determined. Or maybe relentless was a better word. Again, how else could I survive in New York City, trying to be a paying stage actress, which is basically an oxymoron? I had arrived in Manhattan at eighteen, starry-eyed and hungry for success. Eight years later I think hungry was just more accurate.

But I wasn't going to give up.

After I tended to a table of tourists with rowdy kids and an elderly couple, I passed back by the bar, where Grant always sat. He handed me his credit card in a practiced rhythm between us. When he was done eating, he always got antsy to go and I knew not to keep him waiting. His fingers would drum on the countertop.

I knew nothing about him other than his name and that he had a whole closet full of tailored suits. And that he sort of, maybe, liked chocolate chip pancakes. But even that was doubtful.

Behind the counter I ran his card, then put it down with a flourish. "You have a happy hump day."

I waited for him to say thanks, ignoring my cheesy comment as he always did.

But instead he paused as he stood up. "Leah?"

My eyebrows shot up. That was a break in our routine. "Yes?"

He shook his head a little, looking bemused. "Take care."

He had for sure never said that before. "Of course. Thanks. You, too."

It wasn't until he'd already made his way to the door that I realized instead of the usual ten-dollar cash tip he always left me, there was a hundred-dollar bill sitting under his coffee cup. Clearly, he was distracted and had given me the wrong bill from his wallet. I couldn't in good conscience take ninety bucks more than his standard tip.

"Theresa," I said, grabbing the hundred-dollar bill and sprinting from behind the counter. "Cover me for two seconds."

"Where are you going?" she asked, turning from a table with

an elderly couple.

"Grant forgot something," I said, waving the money in the air and glancing out the windows to see if he had gone right or left.

Darting around a young guy entering the diner, smoothing down his hair, I burst out of the front door and onto Broadway. It was a beautiful fall morning, temperatures mild, sun shining. I love early October in the city. The sweaty stench of summer has passed and a crisp breeze blows in.

But there was no time to take a deep breath because I could see Grant down the block already. The man had a long stride because he was smoking me. I took up a jog. "Grant!"

My voice got lost under the blast of a taxi horn.

Grant crossed the street. I maneuvered in and out of tourists walking at a snail's pace and cut between a pole and a newsstand. I spotted Grant again fifty feet ahead of me. "Grant!"

He paused and turned slightly, glancing around. I waved my hand desperately at him. I jogged into the street, eyes trained on my target.

Rookie mistake.

Never step into the street without looking.

I heard the horn but it was too late. A screech of brakes wailed at the same time I felt the cab tap the edge of my thigh. Then I was tumbling backward before I could even open my mouth and tell off the cab driver.

Hitting the curb hard, pain jolted through my ass and my elbow. Water splashed over my arm and I lay there stunned, watching people walk past me without stopping. Just legs, moving left and right without slowing.

Knowing I needed to get out of the way of further danger, I put my palms on the curb and started to haul myself up when a familiar face appeared in front of mine. It was Grant, looking worried.

Then suddenly he was dragging me to my feet and pulling me up against that crisp suit.

"Leah, are you okay?"

Before I could answer, the cab driver was leaning out his window and screaming obscenities at me. "Get the fuck out of the way!"

Grant lifted me onto the sidewalk gently, then turned. His fist slammed onto the roof of the cab. "Watch where you're going!"

Then he turned back to me and ran his hands from my shoulders down my arms, concern all over his face.

My ankle was throbbing, my tailbone was stinging, and my elbow felt like a tiny man was inside it chipping away at the bone with an ice pick, but at the same time, Grant's touch sent goose bumps down my arms.

"I think my ass is broken," I said.

Leah looked more stunned than injured, so I sighed with relief. "Asses will heal," I told her, amused by her response. "You scared the shit out of me, do you know that? What were you doing?"

I was almost positive she'd been running after me, calling my name. When I'd seen her step into traffic and get nailed, my heart had almost stopped. I was not expecting to see the adorable waitress from the diner almost die today.

Leah held up a hundred-dollar bill clenched in her fist. "You accidentally left me a hundred instead of a ten."

Shit. She'd nearly died because of that? I'd left the inflated tip on purpose because I'd made the decision I was never going back to the diner again. My attraction to Leah had been growing steadily every single week until I now ate my pancakes every Wednesday fantasizing about stripping her out of her poodle skirt and licking syrup off of her naked body.

It had started out as a temptation and a way to prove to myself I had willpower. I always wanted ways to push my self-discipline and Leah, from the first minute I'd laid eyes on her, had become a serious test. I was supposed to be gaining ground on the distraction. That was the point of subjecting myself to Leah's presence every week.

I don't even like breakfast food.

But instead of my lust dissipating by the strength of my will, Leah had gradually gone from the cute girl I was attracted to, to a full-blown obsession.

I couldn't stop thinking about her. I ate and listened to every word that crossed her lips. I watched her wait on her tables with a cheerful smile. I heard her laugh no matter where she was in the restaurant. I knew the sway of her hips and the swing of her ponytail. I had dreams about her singing voice.

Shit had gotten out of control. I had failed. Lost the battle against my cock. I was raising the flag.

There were only two options available to me at that point— either do something about the lust or stop exposing myself to temptation.

It wasn't even a question what I *wanted* to do.

I wanted to take Leah home and hear her hit a high note with me inside her.

But. Damn it. The "but."

Reality. I didn't do relationships. Not even dating. It would be different if I'd met her out at a bar or on a dating app and she was down for some fun. But Leah flirted with me in a way that was so goofy I didn't think that she had any desire in a hookup, so I'd decided it was time to remove myself from the situation. Even if I was wrong and she would happily get naked with me, Leah made me feel way out of control. I wasn't sure one night in bed with her would do anything more than stoke my desire.

Then where the hell would I be? Stoked was not the answer.

Screwed was the correct answer.

The tip was meant to be something of a thank-you for inadvertently fueling my fantasies for six months because I was never setting foot in that diner ever again.

In hindsight, I could see why she would think the excessive tip was a mistake given I usually left her ten bucks.

And why, if I told her the truth, it would come off as more than a little creepy. A lot fucking creepy.

As I held her by the shoulders, I told her the truth, if not the full truth.

"Then you're an excellent waitress and a very honest person,"

I told her. "Because chasing anyone down in New York is next to impossible and dangerous as hell." I pulled back and eyed her. Her ponytail was askew and she had dirt on her skirt and arm, but there were no obvious injuries. She wasn't bleeding anywhere that I could see. "Are you actually okay or are you just saying you're fine? Do you want to go to the ER?"

I had a business meeting at ten but I owed her a ride to the hospital at the very least.

"I'm fine," she insisted.

But then she took a step and almost crumpled to the sidewalk. She let out an involuntary cry of pain.

Horrified, I glanced down and saw her right ankle had already swollen to double the size of the left. Her little white sock was squeezing tightly into her pale flesh. "Your ankle is sprained," I said. "You are not going back to work. You need an X-ray to make sure it's not fractured."

"But my shift…" She glanced back at the diner, catty-corner from where we were standing.

We both saw her co-worker in the doorway gesturing frantically for her to come back. I made a quick decision. I reached down and swept Leah off her feet into my arms.

She let out a shriek of protest. "Oh my God, you don't have to carry me!"

"This is easier than you hobbling." She was average height, but very waifish. Her voluminous skirt might have weighed more than her, and I had her back to the diner in only a couple dozen steps.

Leah gripped the lapels of my suit and said, "I should demand you put me down."

"Why would you do that?" I asked.

"Oh, I'm not going to. I just said I *should*. Because I'm supposed to be an independent woman and you're practically a stranger. But I actually really love the drama of this."

That made me glance down at her in amusement. "You like drama?"

"I like an entrance. I am an actress, you know. When I'm not serving chocolate chip pancakes to businessmen." She gave me a smile that instantly disintegrated into a wince when a woman walking down the sidewalk accidently bumped her leg.

I had guessed she was either an actress, singer, dancer, or all three. That was the majority of the wait staff. Another reason I had vowed to steer clear of Leah. I didn't do drama. My entire childhood was a theatrical production starring my mother.

"Did you just get hit by a cab?" the other waitress exclaimed, holding the door to the diner open. "That's insane!"

She usually worked on Wednesdays too. A few years older than Leah, she always had heavy makeup on and rolled her eyes a lot. She was the kind of waitress who didn't even attempt to move beyond a lazy stroll and forgot any special requests.

Leah was always smiling and moved with a quick step.

"Can you get her some ice?" I said, before carefully putting Leah onto the stool I had been sitting on.

"What is going on?" The manager appeared by our side, a man in his fifties, with a substantial middle girth, looking annoyed. "Leah, you have tables."

"She sprained her ankle," I said, gesturing to her foot. "She needs to go home."

"We're really busy," the manager said. "What the hell am I supposed to do?"

His attitude annoyed me. "Call in someone else. She can't work like this."

"Who the hell are you, by the way?" he asked, already pulling his phone out of his pocket. He looked at Leah's ankle and swore under his breath.

"He's Grant Caldwell the third," Leah said, giving me a wink.

The way she said my name made it sound very important and very pretentious. I wasn't sure if she was making fun of it or not, but either way, my name did hold weight in certain circles. My grandfather made billions developing blighted neighborhoods in both Manhattan and Miami Beach in the sixties and seventies. By the nineties, his return on investment was so great he'd bought a pro basketball team, which my father oversaw. My mother came from old money in the Hamptons and spent the early eighties partying with rock stars, snorting cocaine, and spending money.

Then without warning there was me.

Their one-and-done child. Their "holy shit we didn't think this parenting thing through" child. The child they left to be raised by the nanny and later sent to boarding school. Which frankly was better than if I had been left fully to their influence. Mom's idea of affection was taking Xanax together. Dad's was gleefully beating me at golf. When I was six.

Now I was thirty and running the entire real estate development branch after devoting my twenties to proving my worth.

I worked my ass off. I got what I wanted. That's the Caldwell way.

Getting what you wanted, anyway. Working your ass off had skipped a generation.

The other waitress slapped a glass filled with ice down onto the counter and grabbed one of her orders out from under the warmer. I frowned at the glass. How was I supposed to use that to ice her ankle? I meant bring it in a towel or something. The diner used small paper napkins so those would be of no use with a glass of ice cubes.

"I think she missed the point," I told Leah. "I wasn't suggesting ice for a cocktail."

"I could use a cocktail, to be honest," she said. "But yeah, that's Theresa. I'm surprised she brought it at all."

Improvising, I loosened my tie and pulled it off over my head. I eased off her shoe and her sock.

"What are you doing?" Leah's eyes went wide.

"Making do." I looped the tie around her foot and tightened it, leaving it just slightly slack. Then I eased cubes of ice between her swollen flesh and the tie all the way around. I put her sock back on as carefully as I could and tucked the tie into the top of it. "There."

Not bad for an amateur. I looked up from my handiwork to see she was staring at me, looking taken aback.

"What?" Maybe I shouldn't have taken her shoe and sock off for her. Or touched her. But it was a minor medical crisis, what the hell was I supposed to do? Her co-workers weren't exactly jumping on the situation.

She shook her head and reached up to tighten her ponytail. "Nothing, other than that was just the hottest thing in the entire universe."

Damn.

Maybe I'd been wrong about Leah's flirting.

Her voice was amused, but tinged with a bit of awe, and I was very aware of the fact that I was hunched down between her legs. Thank God for the excessive fabric of her poodle skirt because all of my previous fantasies sprung back to life. I could just ease that skirt up and skim my hands over her naked thighs and…

I got nailed in the head by a giant handbag. Stunned, I shook my head to clear it.

"Jesus, I'm so sorry!"

The woman's handbag was the size of Texas and without question had to contain bricks because it was like taking a boxing bag to the temple.

"No problem," I said, rising to my feet slowly and straightening my suit jacket. I wasn't about to admit it hurt like a motherfucker. Leah had been taken out by a cab. I could handle a Midwestern woman's purse.

Given the thoughts I'd been having, it was a timely interruption.

Leah pursed her lips. "Grant, are you sure you're okay?"

Drowning in lust, but otherwise okay. "Worry about you, not me. Let's get you home."

"My manager didn't say I could go."

"You're leaving." She wasn't working on a sprained ankle

because she'd been chasing me down. Hell no.

I found the manager at the host stand and repeated that Leah needed to leave. "If not, I'm going to strongly advise to her that she file worker's compensation."

"She ran into the street, that's not my problem!" He looked put out.

"I forgot something on the counter, so it is your problem. She was acting in her capacity as waitress, tending to a customer. Besides, look at her ankle. It's already double the normal size. Would you be able to wait tables like that?"

"Well…" The look he gave indicated he was considering that question and concluding his answer would be no. Exactly.

I pulled out a business card and handed it to him. "She'll need the next three days off unless the doctor orders more. Call me or my attorney if you have any questions."

He stared at me for a second than just said, "Fine, whatever. Get her out of here."

When I helped her off the stool and to the door, she waved at her manager. "It was an accident, Lou, I swear! I'll get someone to cover my next few shifts. You're the best!" She blew him a kiss.

He grumbled. "Yeah, yeah. Get better soon, kid."

When we got to the sidewalk, I pulled out my phone. She was leaning heavily on me as she limped so I wrapped my arm around her.

"You're kind of heavy-handed, Grant. You know that, right?" She didn't look annoyed. More amused.

"I prefer to call it taking charge in a crisis."

Leah gave a small burst of laughter. "And I do appreciate it. I would be the idiot who would insist I was fine and walk around on a busted ankle all day. I'm my own worst enemy."

The look she was giving me went straight to my cock. Her words floated through my head again—"the hottest thing ever." I thought about all the times she had teased me with sexual innuendos over the last few months and how many times I had struggled to resist the urge to wine, dine, and fuck her.

There was something about her sly little smile, her makeup-free complexion, and her innocent-looking uniform. It was a sexy-as-sin juxtaposition that made me incapable of rational thought around her. She was doing it now. Smiling at me, the tip of her tongue sliding over her plump bottom lip. Despite a swollen and presumably painful ankle, she was flirting with me.

"I'm happy to save you from yourself," I said, voice low, tight. "I'm calling my driver."

"You have a driver?"

I nodded. I didn't use him every day but always on mornings when I had a meeting. He waited around the corner from the restaurant to get me there on time.

"Grant is fancy," she said with a small smirk.

"I'm practical," I told her, mildly annoyed she seemed to be making fun of me. "You know traffic sucks." After a quick text to Andre, I tucked my phone back into my jacket pocket. "Where should I take you—the hospital?"

She shook her head. "My place. It's just a sprain. But I can take the train if you have somewhere to be."

"Don't be stubborn. You can't walk down the stairs to the station."

I was also being stubborn and I was not backing down. I was *not* going to be the dick who left her hobbling to the train. It she didn't want me in the car with her, she could be driven there by Andre. I had a thought. "Did you have a purse at work?"

"No. I keep my keys, phone, and MetroCard in my pocket. It's easier that way."

"Then we're good to go." My driver, Andre, pulled up. "Here's the car."

Leah raised an eyebrow at me as I opened the door for her. For a second she appeared to debate if I was planning to kidnap her, but seemed to decide my intentions were sincere. Which they were. Regarding her ankle and getting her home safely.

Contrary to my family's opinion (and maybe some women I had dated before I had realized I wasn't suited for dating), I wasn't an asshole. My mother always said I was emotionless, but I'm not. I just am very closely in control of them. Meaning emotions. You know, feelings and shit. I had a lid on all of that. That didn't mean I didn't have a sincere interest in helping other people. It just meant I had no patience for bullshit and drama. So even if Leah had been an eighty-year-old man, I would still have been helping the guy home. It was the right thing to do.

I wouldn't be having dirty-as-hell thoughts about an eighty-year-old man though, which would frankly make me feel a lot better about my altruism than I did right then.

"If I make you uncomfortable, Andre can drive you home

solo," I told her.

Leah collapsed on the seat with a sigh and closed her eyes briefly. She opened them and blinked at me. "Get in the car, Grant. I'm sure you have places to be. Walking will take you forever and cabs suck. Plus, you don't scare me."

"Good to know I don't give off serial killer vibes." I slid in beside her. I greeted Andre and then asked Leah, "Where do you live?"

"Washington Heights."

She lived at the very ends of the earth. Or the tip of Manhattan, which was basically was the same thing when you added in traffic. Fine by me. I was thirsty for more time with Leah and now I had the pleasurable feeling that Leah was just as attracted to me as I was to her. "Got that, Andre?"

"Yes, sir. Just give me your address, miss."

She rattled off a street address. It wasn't a neighborhood I went to frequently. My only extensive experience with Upper Manhattan was visiting high school friends at Columbia years earlier. I pulled my phone out and texted my assistant to cancel my meeting. There was no way I'd be back in Midtown in forty minutes. Work could wait.

Me seeing this through couldn't.

"Are you sure this is okay?" Leah asked. "I don't want to put you out. We can drop you off at your office or whatever on the way."

"You're not putting me out. Let me be nice to you." I gave her a smile. "It's my fault you're injured."

"True." She reached into the pocket of her skirt. "That reminds me, here's your money."

I held up my hand. "Keep it for ice packs and ankle wraps."

"I can't accept it," she said, trying to shove the money at me.

I moved my hands everywhere in evasive tactics so she couldn't press the hundred-dollar bill into my hand. At first, she was frustrated trying to follow my movements, then she laughed.

"What are we, twelve? What are you doing?"

She tried it again, but I maneuvered like LeBron James getting past a defender.

"I'm not taking it, Leah. Forget it."

"Heavy-handed. Told you."

"And you appear to be stubborn."

"Determined, not stubborn."

"Just like I'm a leader, not heavy-handed."

Leah rolled her eyes at me. They were a deep, rich brown, with flecks of gold around the pupils. The first thing I'd noticed about Leah six months earlier was that she walked with a bounce so that her ponytail swung. Then when she had turned, the second thing I had noticed was her soulful eyes. They told a story every time she looked at me. I could tell when she was in a good mood, when she was tired, and when she was curiously assessing me.

That was what she was doing now. Assessing me.

"So, Grant, what do you do for a living?" she asked.

"I run a real estate development company."

"You buy and sell property?"

"Yes. And tear buildings down and build new ones." In a very basic nutshell.

"And that keeps you in pancakes and designer suits?"

That made the corner of my mouth turn up. I could buy a pancake *factory* if I wanted to. "Yes. I have no complaints."

Andre, who was my father's driver for years before becoming mine, and more family than employee, piped up. "He's actually filthy rich, miss."

Leah made a choking sound in the back of her throat.

"Andre, what the hell?" I said, annoyed. "Don't make me sound so damn pompous."

Sure, I was proud of what I'd accomplished as an adult, but I was well aware I was fortunate to have been born to wealth.

"What?" Andre looked at me in the rearview mirror, feigning innocence. "It's true."

"Yeah, but saying that out loud makes me sound like I'm bragging."

"I said it, not you."

Not the fucking point. "Never mind." I looked at Leah. "Sorry about that. I am not filthy rich." I actually was, but I felt compelled to be modest. "I'm just rich."

"Oh, yeah? Well… I think everyone's definition of *filthy* is different."

And just like that, Leah took an awkward moment and made it flirtatious. Her voice was low, breathy.

Green light. That's what that was. And I was hitting the gas and plowing into the intersection.

I eyed her. "What do you know about filthy?"

I had leaned closer to her, turned slightly, my thigh brushing against the fabric of her skirt. Her lips were a ripe raspberry color and she had a divot in the base of her chin that made me want to kiss it. Her chest rose and fell beneath her tight sweater with a quick rhythm, like she was turned on. Intrigued. Contemplating her move. She opened her mouth, gaze sweeping over my lips, and for a second I thought she was going to move close enough that I could kiss her.

Instead, she held my gaze, all seduction and skill, while her hand shot out and tucked the cash into the breast pocket of my suit. She grinned and turned back to the front, smug.

Damn.

"Nice acting skills," I told her dryly. Leah, starring in the role of femme fatale, and I'd fallen for it.

"Thanks. I'm working on eye contact."

I was working on blue balls.

She was cute and clever. Fuck.

I knew a couple of women who wanted exactly what I did— no-strings-attached sex. No one got offended if months went by without contact and it was just as likely they would text me as I would text them. I didn't get… *ensnared*. Leah could ensnare me. It might be time to send out a sexual SOS. I needed zero contact with Leah after today. She wasn't good for my concentration. But I did admire both her boldness and her talent.

"That was savage," I told her. "I love it."

"I need a distraction from the fact that my ankle seems to have a heartbeat and half the ice has melted so now my sock is damp."

Right. Her busted ankle. That was the relevant issue at hand, not my dick.

"You really should elevate your ankle. Turn a little."

Surprisingly, she obeyed me. I dug my way through all that fabric and hauled her calf and ankle up onto my lap. I also tucked the hundred bucks back into her skirt pocket. She didn't seem to notice and just cleared her throat.

Leah bit her bottom lip. "This is weird," she said. "I don't think you want my damp sock on your pants."

There were so many things I wanted to say. All of them inappropriate as fuck.

What I settled for was, "Don't assume what I want."

CHAPTER 2

Was Grant flirting with me? Finally?

Andre coughed in the front seat.

Which made me think the driver heard it too. That gruff, sexual undertone to Grant's words.

For once, I was speechless. My parents wouldn't believe it, since my dad always said I came out screaming and hadn't stopped making noise since. But I was stunned into silence by the close proximity to Grant, his words, and by the pain radiating through my ankle.

We didn't speak for one hundred and forty blocks. One hundred and forty blocks. You read that right. The entire time with my foot propped onto Grant's muscular leg, his tie flapping out of my sock. With my legs spread from the position.

Thank God for the volume of the poodle skirt or this would be more awkward than it already was.

Maybe awkward wasn't the right word. Maybe just... aware. I was just very aware of his body, his closeness, his masculinity.

I waited for him to say something, anything, but he was typing on his phone over the top of my leg. If he wasn't going to talk to me, why hadn't he just gone on his merry way (okay, stoic and smoldering way) and left the driver to take me home solo?

Grant was hard to figure out. He didn't seem like a reluctant Good Samaritan but at the same time he was more matter-of-fact than enthusiastic about helping. He was... bossy. Take charge.

I imagined he would be the same in the bedroom.

The thought made me even more aware of his body brushing against mine, and my leg sprawled over his thighs. As the trip had gone on, he had gradually lowered his arms until they were actually resting on my thigh and calf as he texted. He didn't seem aware of the fact.

"Are you very busy?" I asked him finally. I was mildly amused but enough was enough.

"What?" He glanced over at me. "No, I mean, not any busier than usual."

"You're using my leg as a desk to text," I pointed out.

His arms flew up off my legs. "Sorry. My assistant had some questions." He tucked his phone into his jacket pocket and gave me a smile. "My apologies."

I opened my mouth though I wasn't entirely sure what the hell I was going to say to Mr. Very Busy and Super Hot.

We pulled up in front of my building.

Andre turned and looked back at me. "We're here, miss."

I was both relieved and disappointed. The silence was killing me but at the same time I wanted to scream, "*That's it? This is all that's going to happen?*"

Grant carefully set my foot back down on the floorboard and got out of the car. I lived in a quiet, residential area with brick building after brick building that had reasonable, for New York, rent. It would have taken me over an hour to get home on the train, with people jostling me as they were getting on and off the subway, the entire time. I considered myself pretty resilient but I was very grateful to skip that tedious trip. I could have gotten a cab or a Lyft but that wasn't really in the budget this month. I'd overspent on makeup for the show off-off-off Broadway I was currently in as a backup mermaid. Green glitter eyeshadow is not cheap, even if you would expect it would be. Nothing in New York is cheap. Not even the thrills.

I scooted across the seat and cautiously put my foot down on the sidewalk. Grant was holding his hand out to me, so I took it, needing the tug and wanting the touch.

He gave me a smile that I imagined had gained the trust of business partners and women alike. "Honey, we're home," he murmured. He helped me to my feet.

"Thanks," I said, gazing up at him as he pulled me upright and I found my footing. "For the ride. And the ice pack made from your tie. You were clearly a Boy Scout to improvise like that. I'll dry clean it and bring it to the diner next Wednesday."

"I'm not worried about my tie. I'm worried about you getting upstairs. What floor do you live on?"

I bit my bottom lip. He was going to want to help me upstairs because he was surprisingly kind. And I was going to want to invite him in. Which would be bad. Because there was really only one thing I wanted from Grant Caldwell and it wasn't the hundred bucks in my pocket that he refused to take back.

He wasn't my type. I wasn't his type.

Wealthy businessmen and admittedly bohemian actresses do not have relationships.

But that didn't mean they couldn't have passion.

I kind of wanted to make out with Grant, old school, given how teen my crush was.

I should lie, say I lived on the first floor so he'd walk me to the front door and nothing more. I opened my mouth. My inner flirt won the fight as I told the truth.

"I live on the fifth floor."

"Is there an elevator?"

"No. It's a lot of stairs. Like, a lot." *Subtle*. Not.

"Then let me help you upstairs."

Okay, then. One last question. "Are you married?" I asked as I hobbled to the front of my building. He didn't wear a wedding band but I'd learned that really didn't mean much when it came to men.

Grant actually snorted. "No. And no plans of it, ever."

Aha. We actually did have something in common. I didn't really see myself getting married either. Who would I marry? Another actor who would be competing with me for attention? No, thanks. I wasn't going to settle down, have kids, and move to Long

Island *ever*, so that also eliminated a ton of potential candidates. And a rich guy wasn't going to happen because I'd already spent most of my adult life having an imbalance of power with friends due to being perpetually broke. There was no way I was going to have a sugar daddy talking down to me because he paid for dinner.

"Do you have a girlfriend?" I asked then. So the marriage one hadn't actually been my last question. Sue me.

"Nope. Not even dating someone casually. Why?"

It was obvious he knew why I was asking. His hand was still in mine and he was lightly stroking the inside of my palm with his thumb, the tempting bastard.

"Because I don't think it would be cool for you to help me inside if you're in a relationship. That's getting a bit too personal. And I want you to help me inside."

His nostrils flared. "I totally agree. So that means you're single too."

It wasn't a question. He seemed confident. I nodded. "Single AF."

"I would *love* to help you inside."

Yeah, baby. Dessert before lunch. Could I get any luckier? Aside from the sprained ankle and the lost work shift, that is. But I tried to remember the last time I'd had sex and nothing immediately came to mind.

Then I recalled with a wave of horror. Halloween the year before. I had been dating a guy for a month and I had been enjoying getting to know him. Until he'd passed out drunk while still inside me, then when I had rolled over, he had roused himself just enough to throw up on my back and shoulder.

The memory still made me shudder. I needed that to not be where my sexuality died.

I punched a number into the keypad for the front door. "You know I've been flirting with you for six months, right?"

He nodded, tugging a little on the bottom of his beard. "I suspected something. But for all I know you're practicing for a rom-com audition."

I yanked open the door and tilted my head. "Fair enough."

My "Hi, Grant!" bit every week could potentially lead him to believe I was not entirely sincere. "You've never seemed really into me though. Which is fine. But you're kind of hard to read. Give me a cue."

"Is this you working on being direct? Like when you were practicing making eye contact?" he asked dryly.

"It's not an act. I'm asking as me."

Grant stared at me. His eyes were that rare green that something like two percent of humans have and they were narrowed now as he studied me. His hand came up and he cupped my cheek, which startled me.

The world seemed to recede as he swept his gaze over my lips and back up to my eyes. "Leah."

"Yes?"

"I don't even like breakfast food."

Huh? "What do you mean?" Oh my God, was that my voice? I could hear the breathy arousal in my words. My heart was racing as I tried to puzzle out what he was saying, fully aware and super excited that we were about to have a moment. One of those "cameras zooms in as they stare into each other's eyes on a city street" moments. "You eat pancakes every week."

"I come to the diner every Wednesday to see you."

"Oh. You do?" I was legit going to swoon. Because, what? I had no idea. None. Zero. "But... you don't flirt back."

"Because I am trying to resist temptation." His thumb ran over my bottom lip. "Or, I was anyway."

He was very close to me. I could count his beard hairs if I wanted to. Which I didn't. I wanted to kiss him.

He beat me to it.

Grant lowered his head and kissed me first.

I've kissed men for plays. I've kissed men on impulse. I've waited for kisses, trying to be mature. I've had mediocre kisses and meh kisses and great kisses.

This kiss was phenomenal.

It started off strong, and only got better. It was chocolate martinis and crepes in Paris. It was decadent and rich and had my eyes falling closed and my mouth drifting open.

Grant's tongue swept inside to tease at mine, his fingers caressing my cheeks. I could smell his cologne, feel the press of his chest against mine, hear the crush of our clothes. My body felt like liquid, oozing into him, nipples hardening, a sharp ache blooming between my thighs.

I raised my arms, entwining them around the back of his neck, and went on tiptoes to better align my lips with his. The kiss deepened, went on and on, soft breath and questing tongues. Grant made a sound in the back of his throat, a groan of both arousal and frustration.

He broke away and I dropped back down to my heels, panting, staring up at him.

What the hell was that?

"Am I still taking you upstairs?" he asked, his voice gruff.

I could feel his hard cock brushing against my stomach. His seemingly large cock, thick, like his shoulders.

Um, the answer would be yes.

I knew what he was asking. This would probably go further than a kiss if he went into my apartment. I had absolutely zero hesitation. "Yes."

The tension in his shoulders released and the corner of his mouth turned up in a naughty, sly smile. "I can't wait to hear your definition of filthy."

Whoa. I just might be in over my head. I liked it. No, I loved it.

Now this was spicing up a day. This was drama. This was an entrance, stage left.

"I can't wait to hear my definition of filthy either," I said.

Without warning, he bent over and picked me up in his arms, my poodle skirt bunching up in front of my chest, the unexpected movement making me dizzy. He started toward the stairs and the front door he'd been propping open with his foot slammed shut with a heavy thud.

Grant Caldwell the third was taking me upstairs. Grant Caldwell the third hated pancakes and had been coming to the diner just to see me. I might think it was a load of complete bullshit except I had seen him eat. It was like the pancakes had personally insulted him.

Even if he hadn't been coming to the diner just to see me, what difference did it make? He clearly wanted me now and I wanted him.

He took the stairs like Rocky without the jabs. He didn't even slow down as he climbed flight after flight. Someone did Crossfit and it wasn't me.

"That was impressive," I said when we finally got to my floor and I pointed to my apartment door. "503."

Grant was slightly winded, which was reassuring. Otherwise I might have had to default to Theresa's cyborg theory, because the stairs were narrow and steep. Though beyond the marginally increased breathing, he didn't appear to be struggling. I fished my apartment key out of my skirt pocket and held it up for him to see.

"Can you set me down so I can open the door?" I would have liked to have just hung out in his arms forever but I figured his biceps deserved a break.

He did set me down but he took the key from my hand and put it into the lock and turned. He pushed the door open and gestured for me to enter first.

Which was good, because you had to enter the apartment single file. There was a theme to our apartment and it was "slim." Everything about it was very narrow. It was a bit like living in a tunnel, given there were only two windows at the front and both were behind the closed doors of my roommates.

"Welcome to the glamorous life of a wannabe actress," I said, gesturing to my kitchenette, which was a baby stove, a dorm fridge, a sink the size of a bird bath, and exactly no countertops. There were two shelves on the wall that held our glassware and plates. Immediately to the right of the kitchenette and the front door was the bathroom, which had an odd step up. It reminded me of the bathroom on the cruise I took with my parents at eighteen to Cozumel.

Grant was glancing around to take it all in. That took about two seconds. "Where is the living room?"

"We don't have one. My room was probably originally the living room but they put this wall up and now it's a three bedroom instead of just two. More economical. For everyone."

"I applaud the concept of keeping rent affordable."

Grant looked crowded in the hallway, to my amusement. I opened my bedroom door and hobbled in. The pain in my ankle was bad but not intolerable. I figured I would just pop some ibuprofen, rest a few days, and I'd be good to go. It didn't feel odd to lead him straight to my room because there was nowhere else to go. Besides, that's where my makeshift medicine cabinet was under my loft-style bed.

For the most part I didn't even think about what my room was lacking. It was a place to lay my head, nothing more. But taking Grant into my windowless cave made me aware of how much of a dorm room feel it had. It was what it was. I was proud of the fact that I had managed to survive the city as long as I had. It had chewed up and spit out a lot of my peers back in the day.

Except for the Fab Five. Five of us who had met at an audition at eighteen were all still besties and all still living in the city. Most of the others had disappeared over the years.

"It's cozy," Grant said.

He sounded a little concerned, I'm not going to lie. He was trying to be brave, but at the same time he looked scandalized. He put his arms out like a wing span. "I can touch both walls. Reminds me of my time on the ship."

That gave me pause in reaching into my top drawer of the slender chest of drawers hugging the base of my bed. "The ship?"

He nodded. "I was deployed for nine months."

"You were in the *navy*?" I hadn't seen that one coming.

Grant was removing his suit jacket and he paused to give me a grin. "Don't sound so surprised. I wanted discipline and focus. I grew up with lots of material advantages but no guidance. I needed to figure myself out. And I did."

"I'm impressed." I was. How many kids raised with wealth just went off to college and partied with their parents' money? He smiled and it was a charming, slow, seductive smile that made my nipples harden. Damn it, he was so good looking and it had been ages since I'd been with a guy, and Grant had layers. He was successful, hot, kind, and now I knew he'd served his country.

I so wanted to have sex with him. But my mother's lessons on being a proper host sprung up out of pure habit. "I'm glad to hear you're comfortable in small spaces. Can I get you anything to drink?" I pulled out a pill bottle.

Grant shook his head. "I'm fine, thank you. Let me go get you a water so you can take that ibuprofen you're clutching." He hung his jacket on the doorknob.

I had a water bottle on a shelf that acted as a nightstand. "I'll just use this." I picked it up and took a sip and swallowed the pills I shook into my hand.

"Then you should get off your feet and onto the bed. It looks like you need a boost up."

In order to have storage underneath, it was a platform bed and it did require I launch myself up. I wouldn't mind having Grant do the honors. "Thanks. You should probably retrieve your very crumpled tie."

Grant stepped in front of me. No, he stalked in front of me. He owned the space and his movements. Without his jacket on I could see even further how muscular his arms and shoulders were and I swallowed hard. He put his hands on my waist. His giant man hands practically spanned the width of my body.

He startled me by closing the distance between us and brushing a kiss on the corner of my mouth, and then the other. A shiver rolled through me. He shook his head as he stared into my eyes, looking amused. "I don't give a fuck about my tie right now."

Good. Because I didn't really either.

Before I could formulate a response, he lifted me up and dropped my ass down onto my mattress. Then he bent over, the upper half of his body disappearing over the volume of my work uniform. Oh my God, was he just diving under my skirt? I hoped it was a deep dive.

My heart started to race but he picked up my foot, removed my shoe and sock, then went to the injured ankle. His touch was gentle as he removed that shoe and sock, then unwound his tie from around my joint.

Grant straightened up and tossed his tie onto my floor. Then he said, "Make room for me," and jumped up onto the mattress next to me. He invaded my space entirely.

Given my small apartment and twin bed, I didn't usually bring men home. This was why. I felt like we were two kids sneaking off after a play at summer camp. It was a lot of man on a small bed. The fact that he was wearing a suit made it even more ludicrous. At least I had made my bed that morning though I was regretting the decorative pillow that said "good vibes." I'd had it for years and now it felt like it was further contributing to the dorm room look.

While Grant was untying his shoes (I was no expert but hello, Italian leather), I grabbed the pillow and hurled it across the room.

"What was that for?" he asked, amused.

"Too many pillows for two people."

"True. I'm not planning to take a nap." He kicked his shoes off.

Unlike me, his feet skimmed the floor. Mine were dangling in the air.

"You need to elevate your ankle," he said. "Legs up, Leah."

Grant took my knees and hauled my legs up. I automatically turned so I was positioned along the length of the bed and it just felt normal to go onto my back. I wanted to giggle like a teenager.

A grin must have split my face because as Grant moved in alongside of me, he asked, "What's so funny?"

"This. You. Me. This insanely small bed. The fact that it's eleven in the morning."

"It is kind of crazy, isn't it?" He ran his finger over my bottom lip. "Should we stop?"

"Oh, hell no. I didn't mean that."

Grant laughed softly. "Good."

I just wanted him to take charge. He was being very kind and polite and thank God he was, or I wouldn't be cool with him being in my apartment. But now I wasn't sure I could just attack him. Not when the urge to giggle was so strong. I really needed him to just do this thing. Be alpha.

Maybe he read that in my expression. Or maybe he would have done it anyway. He certainly gave the general impression of being domineering. Whatever the reason, Grant took over. "Take your hair down," he commanded.

I reached up and yanked out my hair tie with more power than finesse. I shook it loose and Grant smoothed it down on my right side, running his fingers through it, pulling it out and studying the strands.

He met my gaze. "You're absolutely gorgeous, you know that, don't you? I've wanted to see your hair down for months."

For being an actress and needing to read people, I had failed miserably with Grant. I had never once gotten that sense from him. I hadn't been sure what his deal was but I didn't think that he'd given any thought to me other than maybe being slightly amused by me.

"I've wanted to see you out of a suit for months," I said.

"Really?" Grant shifted his touch from my hair to caressing down the length of my arm.

He laced his fingers through mine, which surprised me. It was surprisingly intimate. Tender.

Then he flipped the script by tugging my arm up over my head and pinning it there. Desire shot through me, my nipples hardening. My tight uniform sweater didn't hide that fact. I realized how ridiculous it was I had my name badge on. He was clearly having the same thought because his free hand skimmed over it.

"Leah." He undid the clasp on the back of it. "Leah what?"

Who cared? He was driving me crazy, hovering over me, like we had all the time in the world, his grip on my hand over my head causing my chest to rise. But I answered him, because I wanted him to stop talking and start touching. "Romano."

"Leah Romano. I like it." Grant pulled the name tag out from the sweater and closed the clasp again. He tucked it into his pants pocket.

I was about to ask him why the hell he was stealing my name badge when he bent over and kissed me again. I forgot everything I had planned to say, ever, about anything. I forgot I was a waitress, that my room had no window, that I wasn't sure how I was going to afford a ticket to Buffalo for Christmas to see my parents, or that I needed to discuss with my roommate Javier his irritating habit of using my washcloth to clean up his shaving whiskers.

I forgot everything.

All I knew was Grant's mouth on mine and his fingers entwined with mine. There was nothing but right then and right there, him and me in my cozy bed.

His arm brushed mine as he swept his tongue between my lips. It was a hot, skilled, confident kiss. The kiss of a man who knows exactly who he is. It was the kiss that a man gave a woman when he wanted her. It was a kiss that showed no doubt as to our chemistry. His grip on my hand tightened and I reached out and skimmed my hand across his chest. His hard, muscular chest.

As he made a sound in the back of his throat, I yanked his shirt out of the front of his pants. I needed to touch all that hardness. He seemed to feel the same way. As we kissed, he eased my sweater up and caressed across my stomach and waist, exploring. I was trying to undo a button on his shirt with zero luck.

Grant broke off our kiss and eased back slightly, releasing my hand finally. Propped on his side, he said, "Here," and just yanked his shirt off over his head without unbuttoning it. The top button gave way and went pinging into the wall. It dropped between my mattress and the wall.

"Oh, shit, your button," I said, even as I was greedily running my hand under his T-shirt to feel what his suit had hinted at. Hard abs? Check.

"I have other shirts." He reached over his head and gave the same treatment to his T-shirt. He just hauled it by the neckline up and over. He tossed it in the general direction of the floor. "Your turn." He took the bottom of my sweater and yanked it up. I lifted my head and shoulders up so he could fully remove it.

I was wearing a very practical bra because it was comfortable, gave full coverage, and was mostly seamless under my tight uniform sweater. It wasn't unattractive, just not exactly enticing.

I had very average-size breasts, which I appreciated. Not too big, not too small. Grant cupped one, his large hand covering the entire thing. Either they were smaller than I had realized or he had some big-ass hands.

Then again, I tended to date artists, musicians, and baristas, and they were predominantly thin, with long fingers, but no strength. Grant was by far the most filled-out guy I'd ever seen naked. In person, anyway.

He teased at my nipple with this thumb through the fabric of my bra before lowering his head and skimming his lips over me. I felt a deep tug between my thighs. He was barely touching me and I was so completely turned on I was contemplating begging him to get this train rolling a little faster.

Grant bit my nipple.

I gave a startled cry. Not because it felt bad but because it felt good. "I wasn't expecting that."

He glanced up at me over my breasts. "Too much?" Even as he spoke, his reach was behind my back undoing the bra and removing it.

I shook my head as he took down the straps and sent my bra sailing into the air. "No. Not at all."

"Are your roommates home?" he asked, his mouth hovering my nipple.

I could feel his breath teasing over my flesh as he spoke. I shook my head a second time. "No. They're at work." Thank God. I didn't need questions about who Grant was and where this was going.

It was going nowhere but one and done. One opportunity to experience what it was like to be with Grant and then we could go back to waitress and customer.

Or maybe not even that, given he didn't actually like breakfast food.

"I'm glad we're alone, because you're going to be screaming," Grant said.

That was more than a little arrogant. I gave a little scoff. Just because I'd been hot for him for months didn't mean I would spontaneously orgasm. He needed to put some work in. "Prove it."

The smile he gave me made me instantly shiver. Whoa, boy. That was some wicked, smoldering arrogance right there. That was a man who liked to win.

Yay.

"I'm not a man who walks away from a challenge." Grant reached behind me and grabbed another of my pillows, this one fortunately a solid gray. He lifted my leg and rested my swollen ankle on it. "Lie back and relax."

My flirty retort died on my lips when he took my nipple into his mouth and teased over it with his tongue. Good start. Not worthy of screaming, but a solid beginning. He rolled the other nipple between his fingers.

"I've pictured licking maple syrup off your nipples more times than I can count," he murmured.

Oh, my. I thought about him eating, staring at his plate, no phone out, no book. Now I knew why. It was incredibly sexy to think I had inspired contemplations. As he flicked his tongue over my nipple I actually pondered if I had any syrup in the apartment. No, none. That would be a mess anyway. "I always thought you were meditating."

"In a manner of speaking." Then he stopped using his mouth for speaking.

He licked, he sucked, he *consumed* my nipples, my tits. He spent just enough time on one area that I would start to moan and arch into his touch, then he would shift to a different part of my body. It was driving me crazy, though I refused to admit it. The scratch of his beard only increased my arousal and the sensitivity of my skin.

When he shifted, and kissed me again, it wasn't urgent. It was languid, exploratory, suggestive of further things to come. As he took my mouth, he ran his palm over my nipples, increasing the ache that I had for him. For more.

He was in no hurry. Nor did he seem to need me to touch him, though I had at one point started gripping his biceps so I didn't float off the bed to the ceiling. It wasn't long before I was digging my nails into his warm skin.

Grant's attention to my tits, to my neck, to my mouth just went on and on until I started to shift restlessly. I hadn't made out this long since high school and my lower half wanted in on the party.

Just when I thought I might actually orgasm just from his kisses alone, he pulled back.

Staring down at me, his expression intense, he gripped the

fabric of my skirt and hauled it up past my thighs, never breaking eye contact. His thumb ran over the front of my panties, very lightly, very briefly. He slid them off.

Then Grant Caldwell the third got what he wanted.

Because when he bent down and gave my inner thighs the same, slow, purposeful attention, I started to pant. Then moan. I said his name at least twice.

And then, as his tongue worked me feverishly and I came, hard, I screamed.

It might have been words. It might have been a single desperate plea to a higher power. It might have been nothing more than a scream inside my own head, but I shattered so fully and completely that I lost all sense of anything other than my own body.

When I finally came back down to earth and stopped trying to bury my fingertips into Grant's biceps, I took a deep breath and pushed my hair back off my face.

Grant raised his head. He ran his hand down over his jaw, his green eyes darker than usual. "You taste better than maple syrup."

Goose bumps rose on my heated flesh. He went on his knees and undid his pants.

He shoved them down and I knew that I had been right to crush on him.

The man had been gifted with a perfect package.

Eight inches of come to mama.

He pulled a condom out of his pocket and I pondered karma and the irony of having to get hit by a cab in order to finally have a piece of Grant.

Then he shifted over me and I forgot to think at all.

Because that first thrust inside me had my eyes rolling back in my head.

CHAPTER 3

"Fuck, Leah," I said, as I sank deep inside her wet, welcoming body. Her almond-colored eyes were closed, her dark hair spilling over the white of her pillow.

She was absolutely gorgeous and I was dick-deep in trouble.

Because there was no way in hell I had been able to resist Leah.

I wasn't even sure why I had tried.

What the hell was it about her? I'd been with plenty of beautiful women. Supermodels. Pop stars. Socialites. It wasn't hard to find companionship when your family was rich as sin and you have a reputation as a coldhearted perennial bachelor. Women saw me as a challenge. That somehow, they would be the one woman who could make me forget all about my vow to remain a bachelor. They pulled out all the stops, working hard to impress me. Until I didn't fall in line with their plans and there was either tears or wine glasses being chucked at my head.

It was a pattern. Maybe not a healthy one, but what the fuck was I supposed to do? I didn't start the fire, so to speak. Just doing my thing.

But from the first day I'd walked into that diner, in honor of my childhood nanny, and spotted Leah moving quickly with confidence and a perky smile, I had been unable to get her out of my mind. It brought me back week after week and it was driving me insane because I couldn't figure out why. The only reason I could come up with besides her physical appearance why I was drawn to her was that she seemed... happy. Positive. Adorable.

There didn't seem to be an angle to her, nor did she seem to particularly resent her job waitressing while she was struggling to make it as an actress.

My nanny, Rose, would have said Leah had good juju. That's what it was. She had good energy.

More likely, I was bored with the same old same old. I wanted to taste a different flavor.

And as I moved inside her, the taste of her pussy still on my tongue, I wasn't sure why the hell I hadn't acted on this sooner because Leah was fucking perfect.

Her full raspberry-colored lips were slightly parted, and each time I buried my cock inside her, she gave a soft little moan that turned me on even more. "Open your eyes," I told her, wanting to see her desire.

Her fingers were on my biceps and she dug in at my words, deep. Almost like a warning. She did open her eyes but she shook her head slightly. "So damn bossy. You need someone to teach you a lesson."

"You can punish me later," I said. "Right now, I want to see you when I'm fucking you."

Her eyes widened and she gave another one of those soft groans as I eased in and out of her. It had been a decade since I'd had sex on a twin bed, but while there was no room to maneuver, it also created an intimacy between us. Her legs were resting on the backs of my thighs and my hands were splayed out on either side of her head. Nothing fancy. Just two people moving together in pleasure.

"What do you see?" she asked, before biting her bottom lip in a way that made my cock harden even more inside her.

Leah's legs squeezed tighter around me and her eyes were glazed. Her nails were pressing hard into my flesh and her entire body was arching up toward me, questing more.

"I see a woman who is about to come. Either that or she's an incredible actress."

"Oh, I'm an amazing actress," she said, her voice breathy. "But… I am about to come. You're right about that."

She squeezed her eyes shut briefly as she panted, then she opened them and locked eyes with me. "Oh, God, Grant…"

I both felt it and saw it the moment she went over the edge. Her inner passage gave a little squeeze to my cock and her mouth flew open on a sharp cry.

It was a total turn-on and had me following right behind her.

I thrust harder, faster, until I was gritting my teeth. Her twin bed was creaking as I exploded.

Damn. It was intense, and super fucking satisfying. I let out a deep sigh as I came to a rest, leaning my weight a little on Leah.

"That was fun," she said.

I nodded. "To understate it, yes. That was definitely fun." I ran my thumb over her lip before giving her a soft kiss. "You're amazing."

"You're enjoyable yourself."

Rolling off of her, I tried to find a place to go but the bed was too small. I was on my side but there was nowhere for my arm to lie but right over her chest. My leg was crushing hers. And I could basically eat her ear if I wanted to. It was hot in the tiny room and I wasn't going to last long in this position. The intimacy of sex retreated to crowded, but it was more amusing than annoying. "This bed was not made for two people."

Since my hand had nowhere to go but on her tit, I teased at her nipple just because I could.

She actually picked my hand up and moved it off of her nipple and down onto her stomach. My wrist twisted at an awkward angle. I didn't want to move too soon to get out of the bed and look like a complete dick, but this was not enjoyable cuddling. It was like trying to spoon in a car trunk.

"Grant."

"Yes?"

"You need to get off of me. I'm so freaking hot right now." She gave my arm a gentle but firm shove. "Seriously, get off."

I gave a laugh. "Damn. No problem. But there is nowhere for me to go, you do realize that. I'm crammed against the wall. So you have to get out of bed first or I'll have to climb over top of you and if I do that, you're going to find yourself with me inside you again." There was no way I could slide over her soft and sexy body and not want another taste.

"I'm not opposed to that."

I liked the sound of interest in her voice. "I thought you were hot. And you wanted me off of you," I said.

"Don't twist my words around. Those are two totally different things." Then she picked my hand up yet again and returned it to her nipple.

That was all I needed to get hard again. I wasn't sure how the hell I was going to do a condom switch though. I'd have to fish my pants off the floor and that might risk shattering the mood. Besides, I was ninety-five percent sure that had been the only condom I had. Not as prepared as I would like to think I was. I decided to just focus on getting Leah off again. That would be satisfying as hell.

I gave her a slow kiss as I shifted over top of her. "How is this? Are you getting hot?" Skimming my hand down her soft naked body, I eased a finger inside her. She let out a little sigh of pleasure.

"I'm very hot. And if I'm going to be this hot, I might as well have an orgasm."

"Sounds efficient to me." I watched her face as I stroked, testing what angle and speed brought out the most positive reaction from her. Leah was expressive, which wasn't surprising given her chosen career path.

It was easy to see when I hit the sweet spot. Her back arched, her hips fell apart, and she gasped, her eyes widening. "Very, very hot..." she murmured.

Working with a steady rhythm, I moved in and out of her, retreating to skim her clit, enjoying the way she started to move her hips in harmony with my finger.

"I thought..." she said, words trailing off as she reached for me, trying to find my cock. "You were..."

"I don't have another condom."

"Don't let that stop you." Leah's arm shot up behind her and she fumbled around. When I was about to ask what the hell she was doing and tell her hell yes, not having a condom was definitely going to stop me, she pulled her hand back out from under her pillow.

She waved a condom at me.

Oh, fuck, it was akin to a matador waving a red blanket. I paused with my finger inside her, not wanting her to come if I was being given another opportunity to do more. "You keep condoms under your pillow? I'm damn impressed and grateful as hell."

"It's a small room," she said. "Storage is at a premium. Besides, it's convenient."

I took the packet from her. "You're the wisest woman in the world."

She laughed. "Calm down."

"No." I did what I needed to do to switch the condoms and I cupped her cheek as I tasted her lips. "I can't calm down when your naked body is inches from mine."

It shouldn't have surprised me that Grant was intense in bed. I only had to think about the way he ate his pancakes to realize that the same single-minded determination would apply to sex as well. He made eye contact consistently. He watched me, and adjusted his strokes based on my reaction.

He had pulled my left leg up, holding it against his chest, so that this time when he thrust into me, it was even deeper than before. I didn't think I could get any more turned on, but yep. He proved me wrong.

It was ridiculously stuffy in my room but I didn't even care. It felt right to be in a confined space, warm skin on warm skin, nowhere to spread out, the ceiling low. It made it intimate, sensual, especially since it was midday. There was no sense of light or time in my small room. There was nothing else but these few stolen moments of mutual pleasure.

My orgasm took me by surprise. It just slammed into me when Grant hit just the right angle and I cried out, hands splayed across his muscular chest. "Yes, that's so good."

He squeezed my ankle convulsively, his expression fierce as he followed me with his own explosion. "Damn," he breathed.

Grant sat back and put his hands on his thighs as he caught his breath. "That was hot as hell. Leah, you're the best waitress I've ever had."

That made me laugh. "I try to be accommodating."

"I've been accommodated to within an inch of my life." Grant rubbed the back of his head, which gave me a view to die for.

He was all glistening muscles and manly beard. Strong thighs and ripped biceps. He didn't have any tattoos that I could see, but that didn't surprise me. He was very Wall Street, despite the beard. It seemed to be his only nod to being under thirty-five.

"What?" he asked, eyebrows rising.

I shook my head. "Nothing. I'm just checking you out. You wear naked well, Grant."

"So do you." Grant stretched his arms over his head and swung his legs around. "I need to see what time it is. I have a meeting I can't miss."

I couldn't even blame the lack of hang-out space in the apartment. Even if I had a full living room and a kitchen crammed with snacks, Grant didn't seem like the settle-in-for-the-day type. Which was totally fine. I wasn't even sure I'd want to have him linger. It had been perfect, just the way it was, and I didn't want to risk tainting that in any way. I didn't want expectations of any kind.

"I understand. You can take a shower if you want." He would look like King Kong in a Tardis doing it, given the small scale of our shower, but he might enjoy some cold water.

"Thanks, I appreciate it, but I'm going to run home for a new shirt so I can jump in the shower there." Grant had jumped down and was scooping up his clothes and tossing them on the bed so he could get dressed. He gave me a grin. "I seem to be missing a button."

I suspected that button was somewhere under my bed lost in a pile of dust. "Sorry about that. But not really," I said.

"You don't sound at all sorry. But I forgive you." He gave me a dirty smile. "Because I'm not sorry either." He pulled on his pants and shoved his arms in his sleeves.

I tried to remember if I'd ever been with a guy who wore a suit before sex and I didn't think I had. Prom didn't count because that had been a rental tux and my high school boyfriend, Dante, had been very uncomfortable in anything other than a basketball uniform. He hadn't removed his jacket with smooth moves. More like a giraffe trying to shake off a blanket.

Grant looked like he'd been an infant in a blazer. He'd probably learned to do his own tie by the first grade.

"Can I get you anything before I leave?" Grant asked, leaning against my bed as he buttoned up his shirt. "I don't want you walking around too much on that ankle."

"No, I'm good." I felt lazy and content and I had no intention of moving anytime soon. "I'm going to lay in bed naked and watch YouTube videos."

He made a growling sound in the back of his throat. "Don't say things like that. And don't look at me like that. Like I said, I have an appointment this afternoon I can't miss."

"How am I looking at you?" I asked, feigning innocence, as I trailed my fingertips over my breasts.

"You're killing me."

"I am the wisest woman in the world, according to you." I wanted Grant to stay, but at the same time I wasn't sure how smart that was. He looked torn, but I could see he was determined to leave despite how amazing more sex might be. I was not about to be that girl who talked a guy into sticking around. More would be better, but honestly, I had gotten more than I had expected out of the day and I was thrilled with that.

Again, aside from the sprained ankle, that is.

"You *are* the wisest woman in the world. You let me upstairs, didn't you?" He gave me another grin and tucked his shirt into his dress pants and yanked his jacket off the doorknob. He put it on with a practiced movement. "And I'm sorry about your ankle."

"It will heal." I rolled onto my side and studied him. "Don't forget your tie."

He bent over and then held it up. "Got it."

Grant turned toward me. His gaze swept over the length of my body and his nostrils flared a little. Then he seemed to steel himself to leave. He gave a groan and pushed back from the bed.

Then he said, "Put more ice on that ankle," before giving me a quick kiss.

As he crowded my space just briefly for that last press of his lips on mine, I was thinking I would probably never see Grant again.

Which was a shame. He really was an intriguing guy. And sexy. And hot.

I sighed, mostly with contentment as Grant went down the hall. I gave him a "Bye, Grant!" in my diner voice.

He gave a laugh, then I heard him close my front door behind him.

As I rolled over to grab a sip of water, I spotted my poodle skirt on the floor. I'd seen him stuff the hundred bucks back in the pocket and I realized I'd never managed to give it back.

He was definitely a man who got what he wanted.

My phone buzzed on my dresser. It was my friend, Dakota, who had been one of my first roommates when I moved to the city. "Hey," I said, as I sat up and answered. It didn't feel weird to be talking to her naked because she couldn't see me, but also, we'd been in a hell of a lot of dressing rooms together over the years.

"What's up?" She was chewing something in my ear that had a hell of a crunch to it. "Want to grab drinks tonight? I have like three free hours and I need to use them wisely."

"I sprained my ankle so I can't really go very far."

"Wait, yeah, why aren't you at work?"

"Because I sprained my ankle when I got tapped by a cab."

"You got tapped by a cab driver?" She sounded gleefully scandalized.

"No!" I set my phone down on the dresser and hit speaker. Then, gingerly easing myself onto the floor, I dug in a drawer for some shorts and a T-shirt. "This rich guy who comes into the diner every week. He gave me a ride home from work *after* I got hit by a cab and well, you know. Sex happened."

"That is a lot of blocks. Dude deserved a thank-you."

I laughed. "I've had a crush on him for six months. This was an opportunity I couldn't pass up."

"Understood. Are you capable of hobbling to the nearest bar by your apartment? I can be there around seven."

"I can manage that. I'm going to elevate it now." I pulled on my clothes and gingerly walked down the hall to lock my apartment door. I had a fear about being attacked in my own apartment like in a home invasion movie.

"Cool. See you later and you can tell me all about the rich guy."

"His name is Grant," I said as I walked back to my room. Then I cursed myself because I could hear it in my voice. I sounded a little too eager.

Like... I liked him.

Dakota heard it too. "Ooh la la, Leah has a boyfriend."

I groaned. "No. I don't. This was a one and done. I swear to you."

Grant and I had nothing in common. It would never work.

He'd left without one word about seeing each other again, which was exactly what I had expected. It had been spontaneous fun.

But I couldn't help but wonder if he would be at the diner next Wednesday.

Eating his pancakes. Fantasizing about syrup.

Andre eyed me as I got into the car. I watched him take in my rumpled suit and disheveled hair. He opened his mouth.

I slammed the door shut. "Not one word, Andre. Seriously."

He grinned. "I didn't say anything."

"I need to swing by my apartment and change before my three o'clock appointment." Not only were my clothes wrinkled, I was missing my top shirt button and my tie. Plus, I smelled like sex.

Andre snorted. "No shit."

"Mind your own business," I said absently, not actually

annoyed with Andre. I was distracted. I was… sucker-punched.

Leah had been everything I had envisioned and more.

My assistant was harassing me via text with questions about when I was going to be available, but I honestly didn't care. I had half a mind to just go home and call it a day. I wanted to pour myself a glass of whiskey and remember every detail of Leah. Of her body, her smile, her orgasm.

Holy shit, that had lived up to every dirty thought I'd had about her for the last six months.

The only problem was now I wanted more. I wanted her in my apartment, in a big bed that would allow me to change positions with her easily. I wanted to see her naked in my shower, and to press her back up against the Carrera marble. I wanted to bend her over my sofa and take her from behind while she made those sexy-ass sounds of pleasure.

I wanted her. Damn it.

I cleared my throat and adjusted my cock.

Dialing my assistant, I glanced out the window at the tree-lined street. The neighborhood had investment potential.

"Where are you?" Darren demanded instead of greeting me. He sounded frantic.

Fresh out of college, he was intelligent, eager to learn, and just as much of a workaholic as I was. Darren was short, thin, and wore designer glasses. He donned bow ties and pants that barely skimmed his ankles with insanely expensive socks below the cuffs. My mother loved Darren and kept suggesting that I should date him, ignoring the obvious that I was neither gay nor interested in the messy dynamic of dating an employee who was a decade younger than me.

But in the end, what my mother wanted was what mattered when it came to her opinions on my life. She thought we'd make a great couple. Therefore, reality didn't matter.

"I'm in the car heading to my apartment."

"Why? What is going on?" Darren made a sound of disapproval.

"I am freaking out. Mr. Zhang is flying out tomorrow. You have to see him today if you want to discuss the Times Square hotel project."

"I know. That's why I'm meeting him at three." I glanced at my watch. Twelve thirty. Plenty of time. "Now don't worry about that. I need you to order a care package and send it to Leah Romano." I tapped Andre. "What was that address, Andre?"

He gave me the address for Leah's building and I repeated it to Darren. "It's for a sprained ankle so a bandage and... I don't know. What the hell goes in a care package?" It's not like I'd ever gotten one. "Flowers, right?"

There was a pause then Darren said, "Well, who is she?"

He sounded curious and I decided to keep it as close to the truth as possible. "She's the woman who serves me every Wednesday and she got hit by a cab chasing after me when I dropped a hundred-dollar bill and she tried to return it to me. Fortunately, it wasn't too serious but she did wind up with a sprained ankle."

I'd already given her my eight-inch package but that didn't count. It seemed appropriate and polite to send her a little something. It was my fault she'd run into the street and was now going to miss several days of work.

"What's the budget?"

"I don't know. Use your judgement."

"I'm on it."

"Okay, I'll talk to you later." I ended the call and almost immediately my screen lit up. My father. I sighed. If I didn't answer he would keep calling.

"Hey, Dad, how are you?"

"Your mother says you haven't RSVP'd to the anniversary party."

That made me roll my eyes. "I will be there. I told Mom I'll be there." My mother just liked to stir up my father. When it came to me, it was easy for her to do. Nothing I ever did was good enough for him, which was ironic given that he'd spent most of his life doing nothing but pursuing pleasure.

The car was heading downtown, and as usual, I felt impatient. Impatient to get back to work. Impatient with my family. The fact that my parents, given each of their multiple affairs, many fights, and even one restraining order back in the nineties, were determined to celebrate their thirty-fifth wedding anniversary seemed both bizarre and pointless.

But I would go because I had no desire to waste valuable time arguing.

"This is really important to her. Just like it's important to both of us that you settle down, too. You're too damn old to be having sex with random women."

Was I? Clearly not given I had just left Leah's apartment. His condescending tone irritated me. "My personal life is just that—personal."

"Not when there is several billion dollars plus at stake. I sent you something from my attorney. Did you review it?"

That gave me pause. "No. I've been out of the office this morning. What did you send me?"

"Just read it. And just so you know, I'm not changing my mind on this, so don't even try. It's legal and binding and I refuse to back down."

What the hell? All my feelings of contentment disappeared. My father was a shitty businessman and impulsive. I had no clue what he had just dropped on me and it pissed me off. "Then let me off the phone so I can read it."

"Fine. Talk to you soon."

I didn't say a word, just ended the call and opened up my work email. There it was, from my father's personal attorney. I opened the attached document, enlarged it, and started reading.

"Are you fucking kidding me?" I yelled at my phone, outraged and pissed off.

I used voice command to order my phone, "Call my lawyer, Sam Rothstein."

"Calling Sam Rothstein."

This was complete and total bullshit and I was not going to let my father dictate my life.

Required to be in a committed relationship to retain position as CEO of real estate division my fucking ass.

There was no way that was legally binding.

CHAPTER 4

"It's legally binding," Sam said an hour later.

"What the fuck?" I said. "That's not possible. My father can't use the company to force me to have a girlfriend." It was the dumbest thing I'd ever heard in my entire life.

It was stupid, pointless, idiotic, controlling, insane. Dickheaded, dumb, and not going to happen.

I had Sam on speaker since I was fresh out of the shower and dressing for my meeting with Zhang. Sam had called me after reviewing the document I had forwarded to him.

"Technically, he can. He and your grandfather own the company. You don't inherit your half until your grandfather passes. So your father can fire you if you don't comply with his standards. Your grandfather is retired, so he doesn't have a say in it at this point."

I paced in my boxer briefs in my bathroom, agitated as hell.

"I've spent the last ten years of my life working my ass off for this company! I served my country in the navy. Neither of those things matter? My father only gives a shit that I have a girlfriend?" It was preposterous. Truly fucking insane.

"It would appear that way, yes." Sam cleared his throat. "Look, just trot out a woman. It's very vague as to committed relationship so just pretend to be dating someone. Ask a female friend."

Hmm. That could work, but what a complete pain in the ass. "That makes it even stupider. Why the hell would it be a legal document if the terms are vague?"

"It says you have to display obvious affection and bring her to all family gatherings."

"What?" Jesus. I knew no woman in my friend pool or casual dating circle that I would subject to holidays with my family.

"Hell, in that case, hire an actress," Sam said. "Though you didn't get that as legal advice from me. That's me telling you as a friend."

Wait a minute.

Hire an actress? I happened to know a singing waitress, aspiring actress, hotter-than-hell-in-her-twin-bed woman who I could easily display obvious affection for. "You may be on to something, Sam. Let me know if there is a loophole out of this," I told him. "And call me back. I'm going to reach out to an actress I know because there is no way in hell my father is going to win this battle."

I'd worked way too hard for my current position.

My father was the playboy, not me. I hadn't broken hearts in years, not since I'd learned how to be brutally upfront with women I slept with. I didn't dwell too deep into my parents' relationship anymore because I didn't understand it and no longer cared to, but rumor had it my mother had set my father's Porsche on fire because he'd had another woman it in, not even six months ago. They did not have an open marriage or any sort of agreement other than they were supposed to be monogamous and neither could quite swing it.

So this was just straight-up bullshit.

Was this Dad's weird way of expressing regret? An apology for never being around would have been preferable to this. Frankly, the best thing he could have done for me at that point was to do nothing. None of it mattered to me anymore. I was who I was and I was okay with it.

It's not like I would be the first thirtysomething-year-old workaholic man with commitment issues. Half of the guys in my gym were some version of the same.

I ended the call with Sam and went over to where I had tossed my pants I'd been wearing earlier in the day onto an ottoman in the corner of my bathroom. I dug in the pocket and retrieved the name badge I'd removed from Leah's sweater. I wasn't sure why I'd kept it. I'd done it without thought, more so because there was nowhere to set it down in that tiny bedroom of hers. But now I was glad I had it. I ran my finger over the letters of her name.

I'd broken a steadfast rule with Leah. I hadn't explained to her I was not looking for a relationship before I'd stripped her clothes off. That had been stupid, but I'd gotten no vibe from her that she wanted or expected anything other than a fun afternoon in bed. Involving her in my family drama would complicate our dynamic but I wasn't going to lose my position in the company and Leah was the perfect choice to help me.

Would Leah be willing to do some work-for-hire acting? I didn't want to assume anything about her situation but she did not seem to be rolling in cash. I would only need her to pretend to be my girlfriend a couple of times a month for the next couple of months. After this anniversary weekend from hell, that is. It was a lot to ask someone. But I would pay generously and we had chemistry. It would be believable that we were together.

I thought about the feel of Leah beneath me, the soft cries she gave of pleasure, and the way my cock felt deep inside of her. I pictured her sassy smile and her cheerful insistence I was bossy.

The idea of having Leah at my side for the party made the entire weekend sound actually... tolerable.

Maybe even enjoyable.

I slid open a drawer on the bathroom vanity and set the name badge down inside. Then I called the diner.

"Can I speak to Theresa, please?"

It took almost three minutes—I know, I timed it—but the waitress who worked every Wednesday with Leah finally came on the line. "This is Theresa, who is this?"

"This is Grant Caldwell. I gave Leah Romano a ride home this morning. Can you please give me her number? She left something in my car." Not exactly the truth, but it would work for my purposes.

"I'm not giving you her number, are you insane? You could be a total freak."

"Fair enough. Can I give you my number to give to her?" I knew where Leah lived and there was a million ways to track someone down on social media but I thought a phone call might be the easiest. I wanted to ask her to meet me in person. You just didn't DM someone without warning and ask them to be your fake girlfriend for money. *That* would make me a freak.

There was a pause but then Theresa said, "Fine. I'll give her your number but hurry up, I have to work. Unlike some people, apparently."

I wasn't even offended by her reaction. She had a busy job she clearly didn't love and I was asking for a favor. "Thanks, Theresa, I really appreciate it." I gave her my number. If I didn't hear from Leah in a few days, I'd go to the diner myself or reach out online.

"Whatever," was her response.

After she hung up on me, I got dressed and pulled out my laptop to go over my notes for my meeting with Mr. Zhang. My apartment was a two bedroom in the Flatiron District. I liked the more central Midtown location than SoHo or Tribeca. More affordable too, such as it goes in Manhattan, and I wasn't interested in throwing excessive money at an apartment I didn't own. While the outside of my building maintained the original look of a warehouse, inside the apartments were very modern with high-end finishes. Smart technology. A communal rooftop pool and an outdoor lounge. The usual amenities you expected when you were spending mid-five figures a month in rent.

I'd hired a designer to decorate it because I liked nice things and had no clue how to put them together to make a comfortable but stylish apartment. He'd gone a little heavier on the leather than I would have preferred but I did like the masculine vibe. The desk was a raw-edge wood sculpture and I sat down in the chair behind it, flipping open my laptop. I was dressed but didn't have my jacket or shoes on yet. Shoes in the apartment made my skin crawl. Too many damn germs in the city to keep your footwear on inside.

As I ran over my notes on the projected numbers for the conversion of one of the few remaining office buildings in the area around Times Square to a luxury hotel, I wondered how much Leah's rent was. That had been one very small bedroom. My berth on the ship had been bigger than that. Of course, I'd shared it with a guy from Omaha, and at least Leah had the room to herself, but still, it was small.

For half a second my brain went to knocking down walls and making it a high-end studio apartment before I halted those thoughts. I had other current projects.

My phone buzzed with a text with an unknown number.

If you wanted my number you could have asked before you left my apartment.

I smiled, pleased Leah had responded so quickly. Then again, she was probably bored. Hadn't she told me she was going to spend the afternoon lying naked in bed and watching YouTube? The image of that made me groan out loud. I texted her back.

I was distracted by you naked in bed.

You could have waited until next Wednesday.

That wouldn't give me enough time before the weekend

anniversary party to convince her to go to the Hamptons with me.

I have something I want to ask you.

So ask.

In person.

I whirled my chair around so I could see out the large window of my office. The view was of Madison Square Park and it was bustling on the fall day. When Leah didn't respond right away, I texted her again.

Let me see you tomorrow.

I have play practice.

Where is the theater? I'll meet you there.

I'm not having sex with you in the dressing room.

That made me laugh out loud. I hadn't even thought about how my request would sound.

I wish you would, though that wasn't my original plan. I really did just want to talk to you, but thanks for putting the idea in my head.

She sent me an eyeroll emoji.

Since she wasn't saying yes and she wasn't saying no, I pushed.

What time tomorrow? What theater?

She responded with an address and seven p.m.

Then she texted, "Bossy."

I smiled.

Persistent.

She didn't respond, which didn't surprise me. I was probably tempting her to send another eyeroll emoji.

I called my buddy Trevor, who was a talent agent. "Hey, how

much do theater actresses make an hour?"

"Why, are you hiring a girlfriend, loser?"

"As a matter of a fact, yes."

"Shut the fuck up." The wind was rustling and it was clear he was walking outside. Horns blew in the background. "You cannot be serious."

"Wish I wasn't." I gave him the lowdown on the current situation with my father. Trevor and I had gone to boarding school together. He knew my family situation and I knew his. The gay son of a former NBA star, he was no stranger to familial expectations and complicated relationships. "I found a loophole and I'm taking it, so not a word to anyone about this. As far as you know, I'm really fucking into this girl and you think we're a great couple."

"That's really messed up, even for your family. I don't even understand why your parents care."

"That is the thirty-billion-dollar question. Now give me some numbers. I don't want to insult her."

"Give me parameters. I'm assuming you'll be kissing and whatnot. But is there on-screen nudity?"

"What?" Instantly my mind went to Leah in her bed just hours earlier, stretching, her breasts rising and beckoning to me. "What do you mean?"

"Will there be a situation in which she has to make it look authentic? Like posing for Sunday morning bed pics for social media where she's mostly naked next to your mostly naked ugly ass. That calls for a pay increase."

"I hadn't thought that far, but that's a damn good idea." A big bed. A California king that I could roll around in with Leah, taking her every which way I could…

Damn it. My head wasn't on straight. Too much pleasure in the middle of a business day. I needed to get it together before my meeting.

"Got it. So partial nudity." Trevor gave me a number. "If I were you, I'd give her a script to follow and a character to play. Don't just stroll into this cold without a plan."

He had a good point. "You're good at this lying game."

"Made a career out of dealing with actors. Trust me, I've seen a lot of ego and plenty of bullshit."

"You and me both. Speaking of, I have a meeting I need to prepare for so I'll talk to you later. Thanks for the info, I appreciate it."

"Good luck with deceiving your parents."

That made me laugh. "Desperate times, man."

We ended the call and I turned back to my notes on the Times Square project. I was in for a busy night. Trevor was right. I needed to create a character for Leah to play. Mostly the real her, because I thought she was pretty amazing as is, but with knowledge about my life and family.

I called Darren. "Did you send that care package?"

"Yes, it should be arriving by four p.m."

"Cool."

What actress could resist both a paycheck and a gift? "What was in it, by the way? So I don't sound clueless if she mentions it."

I was only half listening to Darren as I spun my chair. Then I sat straight up. "You sent her *what*? What the fuck!"

"What? What's wrong with that? You said send your mistress something to make her feel better and that there was no budget."

"I never said mistress. I don't have a mistress." Who the hell had said I had a mistress? What, was I seventy? This had to be the straight-up strangest day I'd had in a long time. Not bad. But very strange. I couldn't even remember what I had said to Darren that would give him the impression I had a woman I paid to fuck. "Can you cancel the delivery?" Leah was going to think I was a complete asshole.

"I can call and find out but it's probably already out for delivery. I was trying to be efficient. I'm really sorry, Mr. Caldwell." My assistant sounded miserable and mortified. "You said she serves you every Wednesday and I thought…"

I was almost tempted to laugh. "She's my *waitress* at the diner every Wednesday."

Darren made a strangled sound of mortification. "Oh, shit. You can fire me. I deserve it."

"I'm not firing you. Don't be dramatic. Next time, I'll be more specific. Now I'll talk to you later, I'm late for my meeting."

"You can't be late to that meeting."

"I know, that's why I have to go."

I ended the call and went for my suit jacket, pondering how in the hell I was supposed to apologize to Leah for accidentally sending her a sex toy.

"I know I said I would meet you at the bar but can you just pop up to my apartment for a sec? I need your opinion on a delivery I got today." I eyed the package in question with huge suspicion. Why the heck would Grant send me a box? The return address had his full name and an apartment somewhere in Midtown.

"Oh, I plan to give you my opinion on your hookup," Dakota said. "Though I don't see why we can't do that over a drink."

"Not *his* package." I didn't need outside opinions on *that*. *That* was phenomenal. "The package he just sent me via bicycle deliveryman."

"What, is it flowers or something? That seems a little aggressive."

"It's not flowers." The box was the wrong shape. I had no idea what it could be.

"Well, what is it?"

"I haven't opened it yet."

"Why the hell not?"

"Because it's weird, right? Isn't it weird? I've never had a guy send me a package hours after we hooked up. What if it's something psycho? I will be really sad if Grant turns out to be psycho." That would kill the afterglow, which, I wasn't going to lie, I was still enjoying hours later.

"Does it smell like a severed head? Because I think you should just call the police instead." Dakota didn't sound particularly concerned. Clearly, she thought I was overreacting.

"I don't know what a severed head smells like."

"I don't either, but I mean, I'm sure it smells bad. Like death."

I bent over the box and sniffed. It smelled like cardboard and a hint of something floral. Maybe it was flowers. "It might be flowers."

"Oh my God, just open it. Grant isn't being weird, you are. I'm downstairs, by the way. Buzz me in."

I hit the button to let Dakota in, relieved she was going to be there when I opened the box. I was intrigued, yes. Unnerved, also yes. Grant said he had a question to ask me. In person. I was never involved with guys like Grant. Confident, wealthy, demanding. I had no clue what to expect and I'd been very tempted to tell him I couldn't see him the next day, out of pure preservation, but at the same time I was too damn curious to say no.

Dakota swept into my apartment the way she always did, with a booming voice and swinging blonde hair. "Open that box before I die of curiosity." She followed me into my room as I hobbled carefully on my sprained ankle.

The delivery was on my bed so I held it up and then said, "I'm going in." It felt maybe a little dramatic. Dakota was right—I was probably super overreacting. I ripped it open. Inside was another gift box. Inside that were some drugstore supplies meant to help with my ankle.

Not weird at all.

There was a note that was printed, not handwritten. "Hope you feel better soon." It was just signed "G."

"It's a bandage for my ankle." I pulled that out, along with a gel pack that was meant to go in the freezer for swelling. "That's sweet and very normal."

"See? When are you so paranoid? That's totally normal."

And then it got not normal. Because under the initial ankle assist aids was another aid entirely. "Um. Wow. Like, just wow."

"What?" Dakota crowded me and peered into the box. "Is that a vibrator?"

It most definitely was a vibrator. In a box, brand new. Sparkly. Hot pink. Very large. "Yes. Why the hell would he send me a vibrator?" I didn't even know how to comprehend that. "Who does that after one afternoon together?"

"I have no idea but look at this thing. This is top of the line. I'm jealous. I could use this." Dakota picked up the box and studied it. "Seven speeds and a remote. Nice. Hey, there's something else in here too." She pulled out a velvet rectangular box and gave it to me.

I flicked it open, my brain telling me the box was suggestive of a fancy pen. Like the kind my father got when he logged in thirty years at his company.

It definitely wasn't a pen. It was a diamond bracelet. "Holy…" I instinctively lifted it up out of the box and stared at it as it dangled in front of me.

"Is that real?" Dakota asked.

"I don't know, I'm not a jeweler." It sure looked real though. Panicked, I dropped it, tossing it back in the large box, not the jewelry case it had come in. "Dakota, I think I'm a hooker and I don't know it!"

She let out a crack of laughter.

I glared at her.

She stopped and looked contrite. "Sorry. But why does this make you a hooker? I don't understand."

"Because I had sex with Grant and he refused to take back the hundred bucks he tipped me at the diner. And now this. Who else do you give a hundred dollars, a vibrator, and diamonds too?" I didn't even know how to feel about it. It wasn't exactly a compliment, though maybe it was. He must have enjoyed himself.

"Your girlfriend?"

"We've never even been on a date!"

"Maybe he likes to move fast." Dakota pulled out the bracelet. "It's really beautiful. Maybe this is normal for rich guys."

"I can't say I have any experience with rich men. Maybe I should call Felicia. She'll know. She constantly dates rich guys." Felicia was another of our friends we had bonded with over many auditions as young hopefuls in the city years earlier.

There was a buzzing, and fortunately, it was my phone, not the vibrator. I pulled my phone off my dresser and then dropped it down on the bed next to the box like it was on fire. "Holy crap, Grant is calling me. What do I do?"

"Answer it." Dakota put the bracelet back in the box carefully and closed the lid.

I had absolutely no idea what to say to him. None. But I did answer because the vibrator and diamond bracelet were staring me down. I needed to at least try to get some kind of explanation as to what the hell his gifts meant. "Hello?"

"If you've gotten a package from me and already opened it, I apologize. If you didn't get it yet, please don't open it."

Interesting. Now I was *very* curious. Did he doubt his initial offer or did he send me the wrong box? Maybe he'd combined my care package of bandages and ice packs with a real hooker. Or maybe he'd lied and he did have a girlfriend. Neither of which would thrill me, but I did want to know the truth. "I opened it."

He groaned. "Damn. I'm sorry. I told my assistant to send you a care package. Apparently in Darren's mind, spraining your ankle means you might want an orgasm to feel better. Little did he know I'd already given you one."

"Actually, you gave me two."

Grant made a sound of satisfaction. "And that wasn't even my best work."

I cleared my throat, reflecting for a minute on that. Yum.

I wondered exactly what kind of assistant would think that made sense as a care package or if it was any reflection of the gifts Grant usually sent.

Not that it was any of my business. He could have delivery dildos sent all over Manhattan and it was absolutely not my concern. Right? Tell me I was right.

I wrinkled my nose. I was probably trying to convince myself too hard that I didn't care what Grant did.

"I'll keep the bandage and the gel pack, but I feel like I should give back the bracelet and the vibrator. Though I don't suppose you can return either of those to the store."

"There was a bracelet too?"

"Yep. Diamond tennis bracelet."

I thought he would be angry because that was no cheap-looking bracelet but he actually started laughing. "I didn't give great parameters for this package."

That would be a massive understatement. Now that I knew what was what, it was kind of humorous. "I appreciate the thought but it really wasn't necessary. Like, seriously. Sending me a vibrator wasn't necessary."

Dakota was making gestures at me like she wanted to know what was being said but I waved her off.

"The next time I send you a gift I'll pick it out myself. I promise."

Why did those words make me shiver? He didn't mean anything by it. He was clearly joking, trying to smooth over this whole awkward situation but my heart leaped. Just a little. Damn it. Not good.

Which was why it made no sense when I opened my mouth and said, "I'm more of a necklace girl. And something simple with sex toys. I lose remotes too easily."

Grant made a strangled sound. "There was a remote? Leah…"

Dakota was making a rude gesture, grinning.

There wasn't a remote, but Grant didn't know that.

"Yes?" I asked Grant.

"It's a good thing my meeting is over because now I'm hard as a rock picturing you with a remote-control vibrator."

"Not my fault," I said cheerfully, feeling better about everything. "I'll see you tomorrow, Grant. My friend is here and we're heading downstairs for a 'you sprained your ankle today' cocktail."

"Enjoy your night." His voice went lower. "Keep the gifts. Do whatever you want with them. Just don't let them go to waste."

I shivered because his tone was clear. He really was picturing me with the vibrator. A shot of heat went through my body. "I'll talk to you later."

Ending the call, I fanned myself. "Dakota, I'm in trouble."

"I think this is a classic example of 'you're fucked.' Literally." She grinned at me. "I say go for it."

"He didn't mean to send the vibrator or the bracelet. His assistant misunderstood."

Her eyebrows shot up. "Can his assistant send me a package too? That is one pricey vibe and I can't afford that."

I laughed. "Like a vibrator outreach program for struggling artists?" I set the box on my dresser and ran my hands over the velvet box. For sure, the bracelet had to go back to Grant. I couldn't keep that, no matter what he said. "Let's go grab that drink."

It was a good thing I had Dakota to distract me or I would not have been able to shake thoughts of Grant Caldwell the third.

He was an intriguing man, very different from other men I'd been involved with.

I couldn't wait to see him the next day and that annoyed me.

I needed to tell him no to whatever it was he had to ask me.

The answer needed to be no.

CHAPTER 5

I wasn't going to take no for an answer.

I wasn't going to lose my position at Caldwell Enterprises and I needed Leah to be my fake girlfriend. Sure, I could hire a total stranger if she said no but there were two reasons I didn't want that to happen.

One, we'd had sex already so the chemistry between us was real and could easily be put on display.

Two, I wanted Leah.

Plain and simple. I didn't want to fake date someone else. I wanted to fake date Leah.

Because I found her adorable and sexy and amazingly upbeat.

A lot of women would have been too offended to accept my explanation for the care package. Leah had seemed to take it in stride and had seen the ridiculousness of it without being upset. I couldn't even imagine what the hell she'd thought when she'd opened that box of mixed messages. Darren needed to work on his cohesion skills. One of these things is not like the others.

Andre was pulling up in front of the building Leah had given me as the theater address. I hadn't really paid attention to the address when I'd given it to him and now I stared up at it in consternation. "Are you kidding me?"

"What? Is this the wrong location?"

"No." I straightened my tie and smoothed my beard. "But I bought this whole block. Every building but this one. They are holding out and it's tripping up my redevelopment project. But I plan to win the fight otherwise everything I already bought is useless. This is right in the damn middle of the block." The whole issue was one of those that should never have been a problem and now was a giant money-sucking pain in the ass.

"Just throw cash at them. They'll cave eventually."

"That's the plan." I opened the door. "I'll be back in ten minutes."

"You said that yesterday."

I paused with one foot on the curb. "Fuck off," I said mildly.

He laughed.

It occurred to me I was going to have to pay Andre to keep his mouth shut if Leah agreed to this arrangement. At least to the length of time we'd known each other. He could testify that we were having day sex. I slammed the door shut, annoyed all over again at the audacity of my father's edict.

But then I forgot about being angry because the door to the theater shot open and there was Leah.

She was dressed like a mermaid.

A sparkly, big-haired, seashell-on-her-tits mermaid. She shimmered everywhere her skin was exposed and I wanted to touch every single inch of her. First with my hands, then my tongue.

"Hi," she said cheerfully. "Did you find it okay?"

I nodded, trying to focus. She sounded so polite and friendly and unlike a woman who could give me the dirtiest of dirty thoughts. "I'm familiar with the area. You look very… shimmery."

Leah laughed. "Right? I always wanted to be a mermaid. They lure men to their death, you know."

"I didn't know that. Should I be afraid?"

Her head titled, as if she was considering. "Nah. I have more uses for you alive than dead."

"I'm reassured." I gestured for her to enter the building ahead of me. "How is your ankle?"

"It's swollen, but it doesn't hurt too bad." She tried to lift her foot to show me but her fin kept her ankles too close together. "Anyway, I wrapped it with the bandages you sent and I think it will be fine in a few days. I have the bracelet for you but it's in my purse. Don't let me forget it."

I didn't care about the bracelet. "I'm glad your ankle isn't too bad."

She hobbled across the lobby. "Isn't this theater so incredibly cool?"

I thought it would be cooler torn down but I just made a noncommittal sound. I'm all for preserving architecture that is historically relevant, but honestly, this building was like the nineteen thirties version of tract housing. It had just been thrown up as quickly as possible, with elements that were more cheesy than elegant. The details were akin to buying plastic medallions, slapping them on the ceiling, and saying it was art. It smelled musty and I had no doubt it was chock-full of asbestos.

But I wasn't surprised that Leah would be the person who thought something had value simply because it was old.

"We can go in the back of the theater," she said. "They're rehearsing act two but I'm not in it."

Not the privacy I had envisioned, but I would make do. I held the door for her and she limped and hopped to the last row of velvet seats and sat down with a sigh.

I sank down into a seat next to her. "Maybe you should skip dress rehearsal until the ankle is one hundred percent." It might sound heavy-handed but I was picturing her taking a face-plant in that tight floor-length skirt.

She waved her hand, dismissing me. "The show is this weekend. I have to wear this or I won't feel comfortable during the performance."

"What is the show about? Besides mermaids."

"It's about smashing the patriarchy."

Of course it was. "Cool. I'd say break a leg, but you might take me literally."

Leah laughed, then covered her mouth like she was concerned she was being too loud.

The stage was filled with pirates and mermaids and something that may or may not have been a dancing walrus. Despite the general dilapidation of the theater, the set and the costumes were very elegant and artistic. It wasn't giving a high school production vibe, but it looked very professional.

I didn't like that we were both facing forward by nature of the theater seats. I turned to look at her, and she wasn't even really looking at me.

"So what did you want to ask me?" she said in a low voice, watching the rehearsal.

"I want to hire you for an acting job." I had thought about how to present my proposal and straightforward seemed the smartest way to go.

She turned to eye me, frowning a little. "What? What kind of acting job?"

"I'll pay you generously to pretend to be my girlfriend for a weekend at my parents' house in the Hamptons." There was no other way to say it. I just laid it all out there.

Her eyebrows shot up and her mouth fell open. "Why?"

"Why you or why do I need a fake girlfriend?"

"Both."

"Why I want you is easy." I shifted so that my leg bumped hers and I reached out and flipped the ends of her dark hair. "Because I want you. We have chemistry that is very believable." I eyed her lips. I really wanted to kiss her.

She bit her bottom lip, further enticing me. "There is truth to that. But why do you need to lie to your parents?"

"Because they are obsessed with me being in a relationship and my father is threatening to fire me if I don't produce a girlfriend. I can't let that happen. I've worked my ass off at the company."

"That seems very manipulative," she murmured. "On their part, I mean."

"Very. My parents' anniversary party is next weekend. We would go up Friday and come back Sunday." I ran my hand down her bare arm. "You'd have to, you know, kiss me and pretend to like me. Share my room. The usual."

"I see." She glanced back at the stage. "No."

Her voice was flat and matter-of-fact. It took me a second to realize she was rejecting my offer. "What? Why?"

She wrinkled her nose. "I'm not an escort. You should hire one. I'm sure there are reputable escort services that men like you know about."

I'd offended her and I hadn't meant to do that. The accidental vibrator delivery definitely hadn't helped plead my cause. "I don't want an escort. I want an actress. I know you're an excellent one and I happen to like you, Leah."

Leah studied me. "I can't spend a weekend with you, pretending to be your girlfriend and having sex with you, for money, without feeling weird about it."

Okay, so that had come across all wrong. Time to change tactics. Give the control to her. "I made no assumption sex was part of the deal. It's only two nights and we'll be in my parents' house." We could have sex when we got back to Manhattan and I was no longer paying her because I had already tossed out the window the idea that I could resist Leah indefinitely. But for a weekend? I could manage to keep my hands to myself. Self-discipline. It's my middle name. "I solemnly swear I won't have sex with you so as not to complicate the situation."

She frowned.

"That way you can take a paycheck for pretending that you would be crazy enough to commit yourself to me. It could be the role of a lifetime. Challenging enough to be worthy of a Tony." I gave her a charming smile and pulled the contract I'd had written up out of the inside pocket of my suit jacket. "At least consider it."

Leah opened the tri-folded contract and made a sound in the back of her throat. "This is a very generous pay rate."

"It's because it's not easy to date a bossy guy like me. Even if it's fake."

The corner of her mouth turned up. "You *are* bossy."

"A leader."

She rolled her eyes. "So what would my role be? Are you the reluctant bachelor to my clinging stalker?"

That sounded way too much like real life with previous relationships for me to enjoy that.

I wanted Leah, as Leah. Sassy, flirty, fuck-with-me-a-little Leah. "Hell no. I'm supposed to be very into you and you're supposed to adore me." I gave her a smile. "Hence the acting. It's not easy to adore me."

That's where Grant was wrong. So very, very wrong. He was actually very easy to adore and I imagined he had plenty of women in real life vying for his attention. So why did he want to hire a fake girlfriend to appease his parents? He could have a real girlfriend in a heartbeat.

I tried to picture spending a weekend with Grant and his family in the Hamptons and couldn't quite imagine it. It sounded both amazing and horrible all at the same time. "Am I supposed to be me or someone else?"

"You'd be Leah but you can't be an actress or they might catch on to what is happening. So we'd have to create an identity for you as close to the truth as possible."

I could do that. Easily. But I wasn't sure it was wise. It had the potential to get very complicated because well, I was still hot for Grant. No question about that.

I glanced at the figure he had in the paperwork. One weekend would pay my rent for six months. I bit my lip. I had told myself no. That Grant was far too tempting and far too rich for me to get involved with him.

But this wasn't getting *involved*. This was a job. With a man I was deeply attracted to and had already lifted my poodle skirt for. Or allowed him to lift my poodle skirt. Still. It was just an insanely high-paying job that would require me to spend three days in the lap of luxury in the Hamptons, which I'd never been to. Not exactly a hardship.

My mental gymnastics went on and on and Grant took the opportunity to play with my hair again. When he touched me, I couldn't think, so I pushed his hand away. Unfortunately, I didn't push it hard enough and all I accomplished was dropping it onto my seashell bra.

"Shoot, I didn't mean to do that!" I whispered a little frantically.

He made a sound that might have been a growl before pulling his hand slowly, seductively away. "I need an answer by tomorrow," he said. "So I have time to find someone else if your answer is no."

Hello.

Wait a second.

Someone else?

Well, that had never occurred to me. Of course he would hire someone else if he didn't hire me because he wasn't going to jeopardize losing his position. That was the whole point. I was, predictably and painfully, jealous of the idea that another woman would be Grant's fake girlfriend. Kissing on him and sharing a bed with him.

Who would Grant hire? Someone taller than me, and thinner than me. Blonde. I bet she would be Swedish or Ukrainian, with a sexy low voice. She would drape herself over his chest and give him smoldering looks. Maybe she would have sex with him.

Screw that.

If he was having a fake girlfriend it was going to be me.

"Yes," I said, betraying all my prior convictions and acting on the dangerous duo of poverty and jealousy. Not a great combination but I spoke with zero regret and ringing conviction. "My answer is yes."

Grant gave a smile. The kind of smile that spoke to why he was successful and how I had so easily wound up naked beneath him. I shivered and told myself it was because the theater was cold. Which was a total lie. Not like a sort of tiny, baby lie, but what my grandmother would call a whopper.

Because, really, I was shivering from picturing lying in a fluffy white bed next to Grant and not having sex with him. That would be like falling into a ball pit of fresh French bread loaves and not being allowed to eat it. Temptation everywhere you turned. I was going to want to eat Grant.

"That's fantastic, Leah. I really appreciate it. I'll send over more information later tonight." He leaned over and kissed my cheek the way you'd kiss your grandmother.

Well, that sucked.

Twenty-four hours ago, he'd been kissing a lot more exciting parts than my cheek. What a difference a day made. Today he was all business and I basically hated it.

"Sure."

"I won't keep you from rehearsal then. Have a great evening."

Blah, blah, blah. So polite. It reminded me of before, in the diner, when he'd been an aggressive chewer and I couldn't get him to say anything other than platitude nothings.

It felt like going backwards and I have to say, I didn't like it.

Wrinkling my nose, I said, "Bye, Grant."

He stood up. But then he bent over and murmured in my ear. "I promise to keep my hands off of you. But just so you know, I feel like I'm making the ultimate sacrifice."

Then he was gone and I was left to debate how I was going to get time off from the diner and what I should pack for a weekend party in the Hamptons.

I realized I'd forgotten to give him the bracelet back. I texted him, hoping to catch him. God knows I wasn't going to be able to chase after him with a mermaid dress on and a bum ankle. Besides, I had a bad track record running him down.

He answered right away.

Keep it and wear it next weekend.

Now I was picturing wearing nothing but the bracelet and Grant eyeing me like he had the day before in my twin bed.

This was going to be even harder than I thought.

I was going home on the train when I got another text from Grant with a document attached. No explanation. Just a document that when I opened, I saw was a questionnaire.

It was things like my full name, where I had grown up, what my preferred fake occupation would be, what my family dynamic was, and my favorite childhood memory.

Then I saw he'd given me a dossier on our fake relationship.

This required wine. I stopped at the bodega across the street from my building and got a bottle of chardonnay. When I hobbled upstairs, huffing and puffing because of my bum ankle, I shoved opened the front door and almost nailed Javier with it. "Hey," I said, breathless.

"What's up?" He was microwaving something in our tiny kitchen, which meant I had to do a side step past him. "Is that wine? On a Thursday? You're living on the edge."

Javier was a clean-shaven aspiring fashion designer who was fastidious in his dress and appearance but domestically messy and the king of the microwave. He had graduated design school and worked both in a restaurant and dressing models for runway shows.

"I got a new role," I said. "I need to study my lines."

"That's awesome. What is it?"

"I have to be a rich guy's girlfriend."

"That sounds fun." He pulled a burrito out of the microwave. "What is the show?"

"It's not actually a show. It's real life. A rich guy hired me to pretend to be his girlfriend."

Javier paused in ripping open the end of his burrito wrap. "Sweetie, that's called being an escort. Acting, sure, but usually the ugly old men want a little something-something too, you know."

Damn it. I had known he would say that. "One, he's neither old nor ugly. He's probably in his early thirties. Two, we've established no sex."

"Now I'm confused." Javier raised a perfectly waxed eyebrow. "So if he's young, rich, and reasonably attractive, why does he need a fake girlfriend? And why won't you have sex with him?"

"So I don't feel like an escort. Obviously. And I don't know why he needs a fake girlfriend as opposed to just getting a real one. I think he's allergic to commitment and he just wants his family off his back. They're pressuring him, threatening him. The usual." I set the bottle of wine down on the stove between the two burners. "Open this for me. I have a sprained ankle."

"Girl, your hands aren't broken." Javier bit his burrito. "So when is this happening? Is it like dinner or a wedding or something?"

"Next weekend. His parents' anniversary party in the Hamptons."

"Take me with you. I'll be your stylist." He eyed my jeans and off-the-shoulder sweatshirt. "What are you wearing?"

"Now or to the party? Right now I'm wearing vintage jeans with a sweatshirt nod to the iconic Flashdance film of the early eighties." I stuck my tongue out at him and unscrewed my wine bottle. Thank goodness for screw tops on my chardonnay. World's greatest thing ever after string cheese and online banking.

"You're funny. And adorable. And not wardrobe ready."

I shrugged, pulling a glass down off the shelf and pouring a generous glass. "If Grant has dress requirements, I'm sure he'll tell me. He just sent me a bunch of information." I opened the document on my phone and showed it to Javier. "It's basically telling me what I need to do."

He glanced at it, his mouth moving as he read the first few lines. "Wait, the guy who hired you is Grant Caldwell?"

I nodded. "The third."

"He's a fucking billionaire, Leah. He's very well-known in the fashion industry for dating supermodels for like one minute before dumping them."

I took a giant gulp of wine. "That's reassuring. *Not*. Why would you tell me that? Supermodel I am not, if you hadn't noticed." I couldn't compete with that and I didn't want to. It was a good reminder. If a supermodel couldn't keep Grant's attention, I didn't stand a chance.

"And he's *paying* you?"

Javier said it like he thought I should be paying Grant, not vice versa. "Yes! Don't sound so shocked. My job is to adore him." I decided there was no way in hell I was telling Javier that I'd already had sex with Grant unless he asked me directly about it.

"I am so jealous of you right now. I want a weekend with billionaires in the Hamptons."

"You're making me nervous." I walked to my room, carefully making sure I didn't slosh my wine. "I'm going to study my lines."

"All you need to know is 'Yes, I would love another glass of champagne.' The rest of the time you'll just be staring at your hot fake boyfriend hating yourself for not being able to have sex with him."

That sounded one hundred percent accurate.

"Goodnight."

In my room, I propped myself up in bed and skipped over the questions I was supposed to answer. I wanted to read Grant's section first.

His middle name was Edward.

Of course it was.

He grew up on the Upper East Side.

Of course he did.

He went to the Winchester Prep School for Boys in Connecticut.

Because where else would he go?

He had a nanny named Rose, who was retired and living in Florida.

None of this told me anything about him, other than he'd had a life of financial prosperity.

I decided I needed to get at least one actual childhood story from him. An anecdote. I pulled up his contact in my phone with the intention of texting him. Instead I hit the FaceTime button by accident.

"Shit," I murmured, hurrying up and lying back so I wouldn't have a double chin when I popped up on his screen.

Grant appeared in front of me. "Leah?" He looked and sounded curious. He wasn't wearing a shirt and his hair was damp, like he'd just showered. "Are you okay?"

"I'm fine. Where did you play when you were a kid?"

"What?" He rubbed his beard. "What do you mean? I went to the park and on the weekends, we went to the Hamptons. I went sailing and horseback riding."

"Did you ever go to camp? Did you have your first kiss at sleepaway camp?" I tried to picture Grant having an awkward phase but I strongly suspected he hadn't.

"I did not go to camp. My mother was worried about Lyme disease."

For some reason that made me laugh. "A valid concern I'm sure."

"If you met my mother, it would make less sense. She's not exactly warm and fuzzy."

"I *am* going to meet your mother."

He made a face. "Right. I don't think I'm paying you enough."

"You didn't answer my question about your first kiss. And are you naked right now? I'm just wondering."

Grant gave me a smile. "You wish." He shifted the phone so I could see he was wearing a towel wrapped around his hips.

It was a great view of his abs. I hadn't gotten to see nearly enough in my bed. It had been all crowded bodies and hot skin. "I wouldn't hate it," I agreed.

"My first kiss was with Shoshanna Gold. She was two years older than me and her parents had the house next door to mine. She kissed me in the pool." Grant sat down on his bed.

"She sounds like a nice girl." I had a glimpse of his room around him and it was exactly what I had expected. Dark, masculine colors with furniture that looked like a designer had selected it. Everything looked expensive and well-curated. He lay back against a sea of gray pillows.

"She was very nice to me. So who was your first kiss? At sleepaway camp?"

I shrugged and sat up so I could sip my wine. "No. My parents thought real camp was too expensive. I went to a theater day camp and there were no guys there that were kissable. But the football team was practicing next door and I made out with a defensive lineman behind the bleachers. He was big and sweaty and I thought he was beautiful."

Grant's eyebrows rose. "So you're attracted to sweaty? I'll make a note to call you after my workout."

I laughed. "No, I'm not exactly attracted to sweaty. It's just he was so manly. Well, at fourteen he seemed manly to me."

"Where was this manly paragon? Where did you grow up?"

"The suburbs of Buffalo."

"Buffalo?" He sounded shocked.

"What? What's wrong with Buffalo?"

"I didn't think anyone actually lived there. It feels more myth than reality."

"Okay, Mr. Manhattan." I rolled my eyes. "You think Buffalo is a conspiracy theory? A hologram? Don't hate on Buffalo. It's a great town with hard-working people. Plus, we were close enough to Canada we could go over there and get drunk since their drinking age is nineteen."

"That's a solid reason to appreciate your hometown." Grant lifted a glass of water and took a sip.

He didn't seem annoyed that I had called or like I was interrupting his night. "What was this manly fourteen-year-old's name?"

"Bill."

"Bill from Buffalo?" Grant shook his head. "You're making that up."

"I am not! There are lots of men named Bill in Buffalo." I raised my free hand and ran it through my hair.

Grant seemed to lose interest in Buffalo Bill. "What are *you* wearing?" he asked.

"This is the way every porno starts."

"Promise?" Grant shifted and held up his towel. "I'm naked now." He tossed the towel aside.

Oh, boy. Things had taken a sexy turn. Which I wasn't opposed to and really should be.

I couldn't resist flirting just a little. "I'm wearing a sweatshirt and I forgot to put on a bra."

"You forgot a bra? What a shame. Let me see."

I shifted my phone so he could see my chest. What? I couldn't resist. He was hot, remember? And naked. I pulled the neckline of my scoop-neck shirt just a tiny bit lower so he could see the swell of my breasts.

"Lower," he commanded.

When he used that voice—low and growly and demanding—I got turned on and just automatically obeyed. I dragged my shirt low enough that he could see both of my nipples. He swore under his breath. I let go and my shirt covered me again.

"You're so damn sexy," he told me. "Did you call me to torture me?"

"No, I swear. I called to try to get to know you better. But for the record, I'm torturing myself too, so that should make you feel better."

"It doesn't," he said dryly. "And I'm going to end this call before I ask you to come over and spend the night with me."

A flush of arousal heated my body up from the inside out. "Oh, really? Would that be a bad thing?"

He shook his head. "No. But I have to be up at five a.m. tomorrow, and if you come over, I'll get exactly no sleep because I would need hours to explore every single inch of your body."

I'd started a game without even meaning to and now I had just lost. Because now I was going to spend the night wishing I was going cowgirl on Grant's hard, naked body. "Hours?"

"Hours."

I fanned myself. "I believe you."

"Before I go and take a cold shower, when are you free to go shopping?"

"We're going shopping?"

He nodded. "It's in the contract. You need a wardrobe for the weekend."

"I'm not really a girl who reads things like contracts. I just prefer to roll with it." I'd always been like that and I didn't see it changing anytime soon.

Grant winced and rubbed his chest in exaggeration. "That hurts my heart," he said. "You need to read legal documents, Leah, seriously."

I shrugged. "Sure. I can go shopping this Saturday, though we'll need to keep it on the down low or Lou, my manager, will kill me for doing that instead of working since you told him I need the rest of the week off." Lou was also going to kill me for needing the next Saturday off but I would cross that bridge on my next shift.

"Wear what you would normally wear so I can see the real you. As opposed to fifties waitress or a mermaid."

"I can do that. Be normal. Or at least not a mermaid."

"Why don't we meet at my office and go from there?"

I was allergic to the idea of office buildings but I was ridiculously curious to see where Grant worked every day. "Sounds good. Oh, and I decided what I want my fake occupation to be. Professional sleeper."

Grant gave a soft laugh. "That's not a job."

"It is. You test beds in hotels. I figure it's something I know, right? It's not like I can pretend to be a neurosurgeon or a French tutor. I know how to sleep."

He rubbed his beard and shook his head. "I don't think so,

Leah. Pick something else."

"I'm forbidden to be a pro sleeper? That's a little harsh. Fine, what do you want me to be?"

"Something that doesn't involve a bed."

"So sex toy tester is out?" I winked at him.

Grant's nostrils flared. "You're a very dangerous woman. Why can't you be a waitress? We met exactly the way we really did."

"Boo. That's so boring. But fine. I'll be a waitress. A dangerous waitress." I blew him a kiss. "Goodnight, Grant."

"Goodnight, Leah." There was a pause, where I thought he was going to say something else, but he didn't.

The screen went blank as he ended the call.

I took another sip from my wine and started answering Grant's questionnaire. I got through ten questions when I came to "What is your greatest fear?"

It made my stomach clench. I couldn't tell Grant my greatest fear was failure. That I was terrified that in ten years I'd be almost forty and still living in this apartment and never finding success as an actress. That by that point I would have aged out of even working at the diner because they wanted young and perky singers and women have an insanely early expiration date in any entertainment.

I guess I could always apply to be a professional sleeper at that point.

I typed into the document a flippant answer.

Swallowing a roach in my drink at a restaurant.

That was a very real fear as well.

CHAPTER 6

I was opening up blueprints for a condo building we had going up on E. 63rd when my administrative assistant knocked on the door and said, "Mr. Caldwell, may I come in?"

"Yes." I looked up from my computer toward the door.

Cece opened the door and crossed my office. She had been working for me for about a year, and once she had realized I had no intention of making her my Mrs. Caldwell, she had stopped flirting with me and started working. She had a boyfriend now who was a personal trainer and we had developed a really excellent work rapport. "What's up?" I asked her.

I always worked on Saturdays but Cece only did once a month in exchange for having a Monday off with her boyfriend.

She was frowning. "There's a woman here to see you but she doesn't have an appointment. She's very... boisterous."

I glanced at the clock on my computer. "Is her name Leah

Romano? We have plans at eleven so you can send her in."

Cece hesitated. "Who is she?" she asked curiously.

Time to put the plan into play. "She's my girlfriend."

Cece was a cool, polished blonde who never showed much emotion but now her eyes nearly bugged out of her head. "Your *girlfriend*? *Her*?"

That made me frown. "What do you mean, her? That sounded rude as hell." I stood up and reached for my suit jacket. "We're going shopping and probably to lunch so I won't be back until this afternoon."

I had no clue what Cece meant by Leah being boisterous. What the hell did that even mean? Was she doing a high-kick in the reception area? And what could be objectionable about Leah? We had actually talked again the night before for over an hour on FaceTime while we both were in bed. After a long day and meeting clients out for drinks, I had wanted to talk to her and I had texted her. She'd answered right away, and when I had called her, our conversation had been easy and flirtatious. Leah was cute and playful and genuinely curious about me and my life. Yes, she was farming for info to sell it at the party with my parents, but at the same time, I thought it was more than that. She was just a curious person and seemed interested in getting to know me.

As for her, I found myself wanting to draw our conversations out longer. I had woken up thinking about her and wanting to see her today.

Cece murmured an apology and left. A few seconds later Leah came into my office with Cece right behind her. Not ponytail-and-poodle skirt Leah. Not mermaid Leah. Not even lying-in-her-bed Leah.

This was sexy Leah. I was shocked to see her in full makeup with smoky eyes and false lashes. I'd only seen her hair down in bed and this wasn't the same at all. This was loose, but fully controlled waves tumbling down over her shoulders. Between the hair was ample cleavage, boosted up and together by the magic of her wonder bra. She was wearing the tightest jeans I'd ever seen in my entire lifetime, showing off every delicious curve, and I suspected if she didn't still have an ankle injury, she'd be wearing fuck-me heels.

I'd told her to be herself today. Apparently, the true Leah was a bombshell. Not the fresh-faced, ponytail-and-bobby socks Leah I had been trying to resist for six months. Instantly I wanted nothing more than to take her and spread her out on my desk and do dirty, delicious things to her.

Then she said, "Hi, Grant!" in what she had told me months earlier was her Goldie Hawn imitation and I laughed.

She looked like sin, but she was still silly.

"Hi, Leah." I went straight to her and cupped her cheeks.

Her eyes widened.

"It's good to see you," I said. "Really good to see you." Then I gave her a lingering kiss.

"Ooh," she said when I broke away. "That's a nice hello."

"So you met Cece, my very tolerant assistant?" I murmured. "Not the care package sender, by the way. Different assistant."

Leah looked amused. She turned and gave Cece a brilliant

smile. "Yes, we had the pleasure of meeting."

My administrative assistant was the most rattled I had ever seen her. She looked flabbergasted, which wasn't surprising. I had never brought a woman to my office for personal reasons.

"We're going to grab Leah some things for my parents' anniversary party next weekend. Can you call Chanel and tell them I'm on my way and we'd like some privacy? We should be there in twenty minutes. Then around one, make us an appointment at Valentino for a cocktail dress. After that, Prada for some casual things. Oh, and have Louis Vuitton send a full set of luggage to my apartment for her."

Cece gave me what could only be categorized as a dirty look but she nodded. "Of course."

Given the way Leah was dressed, she liked to be sexy but I thought Chanel was a safer bet for the whole meet-the-parents deal. She could have some fun at Prada then to make up for having to be more conservative than I had a feeling she would like to be. I put my hand on her elbow and guided her to the door. "Let's go."

Leah blatantly looked all around her at my office reception area as we went to the elevator. Once we were inside, she said, "I thought we were getting a dress for the party. Not a whole wardrobe."

"You're getting a whole wardrobe." I pushed her up against the elevator wall. "But I don't care about that right now. I'm mesmerized by your hot little outfit."

Leah gripped the lapels of my jacket. "You're crowding me, Mr. Caldwell."

"Mr. Caldwell is my grandfather. Call me Sexy Beast."

She laughed. "I don't know how you just said that with a straight face. I'm very impressed." She went on her tiptoes and brushed her lips against my ear. "Sexy. Beast."

I felt the force of her words right down to my cock. She was mocking me and I was turned on. Women didn't tease me. Women coaxed me and complimented me and got pouty with me. I'd had women stomp their feet and storm out but I never had women talk to me the way Leah did. It was a completely new experience that I was enjoying.

I was hauling her leg up against my thigh so I could get closer to her when the elevator dinged and the door opened.

Three people I didn't know were standing there clearing their throats.

I dropped her leg.

Leah said, "Good morning!" in a cheerful voice as we maneuvered past them.

"How is your ankle?" I asked her, belatedly remembering to be a decent human being instead of a lust-driven cretin.

"It's much better. Swelling is almost gone and it doesn't hurt. I skipped the heels today though."

"Probably wise." I opened the door for her and gestured to the right. "Andre is waiting for us." I had explained the situation to my driver and had given him a generous bonus to keep his mouth shut.

Leah got in the car and turned to me. "Did you read all my answers? Did I pass the test?"

"It wasn't a test. Just fact-gathering."

"Why did I have to tell you my biggest fear but that wasn't on yours?"

Because there was no way in hell I was going to reveal to Leah that my biggest fear was that no one could or would love me. That I was going to die alone someday. Fuck that. That nasty thought was staying buried deep down, behind the broken heart at twenty and the devastation and anger at twelve when my parents had fired my nanny. Nope. Wasn't going to wade through the emotional shit pile of my past.

"I'm not afraid of anything," I said. That was mostly true. I didn't have phobias other than shoes in the house and I wasn't afraid of anything other than the Shit I Wasn't Going to Talk About.

"Ooh, tough guy," she said. "Cool. I get it. Feelings aren't trending with you."

"You didn't exactly give me a real answer either, by the way."

"Yes, I did," she protested. "I am terrified of cockroaches."

"No cockroaches in Buffalo?"

"Not a single one."

When we got to the Chanel flagship, a staff member was waiting for us. "It's great to see you again, Mr. Caldwell. We have the fifth floor ready for you." She held her hand out to Leah. "I'm Vivian. I'm here to help you with whatever you need."

"I'm Leah, it's nice to meet you. Thank you." Leah put her hand into mine as she looked around the first floor of the store in awe.

I squeezed her hand to reassure her. I didn't want her to feel overwhelmed or awkward.

I shouldn't have worried. Leah was taking it all in, but she looked more excited than nervous. Upstairs in a private client room she happily took the champagne they offered her and sat on a plush sofa. "What happens now? Do angels glide in and sew haute couture on me? Or maybe forest animals like Cinderella?"

"Something like that. Though this is just ready-to-wear, not couture." I turned to Vivian. "Can you bring day options for a weekend in the Hamptons? Leah is meeting my parents for the first time. Nothing red. I want her to wear red for a party Saturday night."

"Absolutely, Mr. Caldwell."

Vivian left the room and I eyed Leah. She was smiling and looking mischievous as she sipped her champagne.

"What?" I asked her.

"You're very cute when you're being powerful."

"Don't say shit like that. It's wrong. Cute and powerful don't belong in the same sentence." I sat down next to her and unbuttoned my suit jacket. I put my arm on the sofa behind her, planning to settle in.

"Do I have to model for you?"

"Yes. I get final approval on what to buy, obviously." I tugged the back of her hair teasingly because all those lush dark waves were way too tempting not to touch. "I won't buy anything you hate." It was hard to believe that I barely knew Leah. Being around her felt completely natural.

"This champagne is delicious," she said, taking another sip. "Cut me off after two glasses or I'll be drunk at Valentino."

The champagne was expensive so it should be delicious.

"Are you the kind to be fine with actually being cut off or are you going to get belligerent with me? How serious are you about this? Because I can be the heavy if you want."

She eyed me. "Oh, I know you can."

I gave her a smile.

"And yes, I'm serious. I'd be mortified if I was drunk at any of these stores. Though I don't think two glasses will cause me to be sloppy, you just never know."

"Then maybe start with setting the glass down instead of clutching it like a baby with a bottle." She was holding it like it was the ring from The Hobbit. The flute was even pressed against her chest.

Leah laughed. "Fair enough. But it's very smooth." She set the glass down on the coffee table.

Vivian returned and ushered Leah into a dressing room. They came back out five minutes later and I sat up straight. Leah looked classy, but very cool in a basic, but perfectly tailored houndstooth pants and sweater. "You look perfect," I told her.

She made a face. "I feel like Diane Keaton is Something's Gotta Give. Which she is amazing, don't get me wrong, and I mean she was banging Keanu Reeves. But it's not really me."

I had no idea what she was talking about. "Okay. Something more you. That's fine. And thanks, now I have the horrible image of you in bed with Keanu Reeves and I want to punch him."

Leah laughed. "Relax. I don't even know Keanu Reeves. Plus, he's too old for me. Isn't he fifty now?"

"How reassuring," I said dryly.

Vivian gestured to the dressing room. "Shall we try something else? I suggest monochromatic with an emphasis on texture, not pattern."

"Absolutely," Leah said smoothly. Then, when Vivian went into the dressing room, Leah turned and gave me an exaggerated thumbs-up.

Oh God. I rubbed my beard and hoped she would like the next outfit or we were going to be there for hours.

Leah returned to the main sitting area wearing winter white from head to toe. It contrasted perfectly with her dark hair. I waited to hear her thoughts on it, but I thought she looked stunning. I did nod approvingly because I couldn't stop myself.

"I feel very angelic," she said looking in the mirror.

Was that good or bad? "Not a word I generally associate with you, but I totally agree."

Leah stood facing herself and locked her fingers together, arms out. Then she stunned me by opening her mouth and letting loose with the first notes of "Ava Maria."

I'd heard her sing before at the diner, but that was noisy and chaotic and she tended to move around while she was doing it. This was her entirely still, in the quiet hush of Chanel, the clothes on her body feminine and matching the beauty of the song. She both looked and sounded ethereal as she continued to sing acapella. I sat there and listened, the sensation she was evoking in me one of tranquility. I was a man who liked action and multitasking from morning to the last second before I closed my eyes.

Yet Leah's voice was so serene it felt like the entire world had stopped to listen to her sing.

It was a hymn that I had first heard sung at Rose's son's wedding when I was ten years old. My parents didn't attend the wedding but they sent me with a driver and I sat there in the back of the church with him, dressed in my designer suit, and listening with awe to what seemed like the most beautiful song in the world to me.

With Leah singing it, it was the most beautiful song in the world.

All my thoughts just seemed to flick off, my body relaxed, and I was right there, with her, in the moment.

The last note trailed off and hung there for a second while no one spoke.

I realized Vivian was recording Leah on her phone.

Leah's shoulders dropped and she lowered her hands. She turned to us. "Sorry. I got inspired."

"That was amazing," Vivian said. "Do you mind if I put it on Instagram?"

Leah looked a little taken aback. But then she said, "Sure. Can you tag me?"

"We'll take this outfit, Vivian," I said. I wanted to think about this moment of calm when she wore it at my parents'. "Leah, that was beautiful. *You're* beautiful."

She waved me off. "False flattery will get you everywhere."

It wasn't false at all but I wasn't going to argue. I wanted to tuck this moment away for later.

They went back into the dressing room and this time Leah

came out wearing fuchsia. It was youthful and sexy even though she was completely covered up. The pants were shiny but wide-legged, perfect for her age.

"We've layered a tweed pullover with a lambskin jacket and pants," Vivian said, before disappearing back into the dressing room.

"I love this," I told Leah. "What do you think?"

"I feel like I mysteriously grew eight inches." She tucked her hands into the front pocket of the pullover and did a model walk across the room.

"I feel like I'm mysteriously growing eight inches watching you."

She laughed, an unabashed peal of laughter that swelled and filled the room as dramatically as her singing had. No matter what she did, Leah brought volume to a room, both in sound and energy. Whether it was balancing a tray at the diner or trying on clothing, she had a spark that seemed to reach out and grab on to my dick and hold me hostage.

"Grant, you're a filthy bastard and I love it."

Vivian returned in time to hear that and she raised her eyebrows but made no comment.

"We'll take this as well. Can you coordinate some accessories and have it all sent over to my apartment?" Two outfits would work since it was just a short trip.

I picked up Leah's glass and handed it to her. "Finish your champagne, sweetheart, and then we'll go to lunch."

Grant had bought me eight-thousand-dollar pants to wear for an afternoon. I wasn't even sure how to process that. The pants were the bomb, don't get me wrong, but I had never expected in this lifetime to own such luxury.

And those were just one piece. It was three pieces per outfit, plus he'd just tossed off casually to "coordinate accessories."

We weren't even done. It was staggering and very cool and also a little bit of what the fuck.

Lunch wasn't the lap of luxury. We went for poke bowls and it made me feel more back-to-earth.

Which then was instantly shattered by cocktail dress shopping at Valentino. Grant had very specific instructions for this consultant. He wanted red, fitted, dramatic, but nothing that would overpower his mother, the guest of honor. Which it seemed to me if he wanted me to fade into the background, red was a poor choice, but it wasn't my parents or my money so I kept my mouth zipped.

I tried on four dresses and he rejected all of them. I was amused to see he didn't even hesitate. I would walk out, he would eye it, and then would give a resounding, "No."

Personally, I thought he sounded like a dick, but the consultant didn't seem to think anything of it, and I didn't particularly care. He wasn't rejecting me, just the garment. I thought they were all beautiful and I would have been happy with any of them because they were gorgeous, but again, I just posed for him and kept my thoughts to myself.

The fifth one he nodded. "Yes. We'll take this one. That is, if Leah approves this one."

"Yes, I approve. The only thing that would make this better would be if I ran across the room and jumped into your arms and you lifted me up Dirty Dancing style."

Grant shook his head, the corner of his mouth turning up. "That's not happening. Not with a marble floor."

"That's very disappointing. Don't you trust your own strength?"

"I don't trust you. You're accident prone."

"Rude."

"I'll tell you what. We can try it in the pool, how does that sound?"

"Do you promise?"

"I promise."

"Wait a minute." I stopped in the midst of admiring how this dress made my ass look better than it was in actuality. "What pool? It's October. Are you placating me?"

"Well. Yes. But my parents' house has both an outdoor and an indoor pool. So bring your swimsuit."

I didn't own a swimsuit. There weren't many options for recreational swimming in Manhattan. Every couple of years my friends and I managed to get to the beach but the last time we'd gone I'd snagged my bikini bottom on a rock and I hadn't replaced them. I made a noncommittal sound. No dirty dancing reenactment for me.

There was no doubt in my mind that if I said I didn't have

one Grant would snap his fingers and an outrageously expensive swimsuit would magically appear but that made me feel weird. The clothes were his idea. Swimming felt like my idea and he wasn't my partner. He was my employer. It was an odd dynamic.

After he handed over his platinum credit card for the dress, we headed to Prada. Grant suggested I give parameters to the consultant myself. I really wanted to tell her I wanted to look like I was a dominatrix in Willie Wonka's chocolate factory. Fierce, but perhaps in purple. Somehow, I didn't think that was the Hamptons house party vibe though.

"Can you make me look five inches taller?" I asked her. "I sprained my ankle and without heels I feel like a giraffe without its neck."

She asked me a few questions then disappeared like smoke. I sat down on a sofa next to Grant and propped my bum ankle onto his legs. It was starting to ache.

He pried my ballet flat off. "Your ankle is starting to swell up."

"You shouldn't take my shoe off. We might never get it back on."

"Then I'll buy you slippers."

I had to assume that Grant was used to money solving a large number of problems and that this was nothing more than that, but I couldn't help but feel... well cared for. It was a dangerous feeling. This was nothing. It was casual. We'd had fun and now I was doing an acting job for him.

But as he gently caressed my bare skin, it didn't feel casual. "I'm a size purple fleece."

Grant laughed. "Duly noted." He pulled out his phone and called someone. "I need you to send women's purple fleece slippers, around a size eight or nine to Prada in the next twenty minutes."

He ended the call. "Done."

"Were you actually talking to someone or was that like when I was a kid and my father used to pretend to call Santa to tell him I was naughty and I'd scream and cry and grab for the phone?"

"That was Darren, my PA. The one who sent you a diamond bracelet."

"Oh, fabulous. He'll probably send me diamond-encrusted slippers."

"Or vibrating slippers."

That made me laugh. "If those slippers show up, I'm not sure I have the guts to stroll out of Prada in them."

"Of course you do. You don't seem like someone who cares about anyone's opinion of her. You just live your life."

That was true. "Thanks for noticing."

Grant Caldwell the third noticed a lot of things.

I leaned closer to him and did something that was both impulsive and stupid.

I kissed him.

A real kiss.

Not for show.

And not a kiss intended to lead to sex.

A genuine, "I like you," kiss.

Because I did.

Like him.

Damn it.

"Here we go!" the consultant said, before coming to a dead stop. "Oh! My apologies, Mr. Caldwell."

"Yeah," I murmured. "My apologies, Mr. Caldwell."

Grant stared at me with those luminescent green eyes that I couldn't read and said in a normal voice, "No apologies needed."

I wasn't sure if he was speaking to me or the consultant.

His ran his thumb over my bottom lip before turning to the consultant. "What Leah wants, Leah gets."

My God, if that were only true.

If it were, I'd start with getting naked with Grant in the next five minutes and end with me accepting a Tony award.

Then having sex with Grant after the award ceremony. Then again the next morning on a private plane while we flew to the Caribbean to escape the last gasp of a brutal New York winter and celebrate my crowning achievement.

Not to be too specific or anything.

"I may have to get that in writing," I said.

"You don't read contracts, remember? I could change it to anything and you'd never know."

I gave him an eyeroll and put my feet on the floor and stood up.

He gave me a boost with two hands on my ass, and while the experience of shopping at Prada was surreal, us dating felt very real.

It startled me to the point where I said to the consultant, "Do you have any champagne? I'm thirsty."

"So am I," Grant said.

I knew by the look on his face he was not referring to bubbly.

I was so in over my head and loving every second of it.

CHAPTER 7

"OMG, that was like your own personal makeover montage," Savannah said, her glass of wine halfway to her mouth. "You're living a rom-com. Maid in Manhattan!"

We were grabbing drinks after my show on Saturday night. I should have been exhausted after all the shopping and the excitement of performing but instead I was wide awake and super happy my friends had all come to see my show and hang out.

It was rare that all five of us were in place anymore and I had a buzz from both the wine and my happiness. Savannah's reaction was appropriate for her. She loved a good rom-com and believed vehemently in happily ever after, which was ironic given that she'd dated a steady stream of useless men, including the last guy, who had disappeared after she had told him she was pregnant. Savannah now had the most adorable six-month-old baby in the history of babies and a successful career as a lifestyle blogger.

She'd always been the "mom" of our group. She held hair back when there was vomiting after cocktails, opened her arms for hugs after breakups and bad auditions, and reminded everyone to drink water between each glass of wine. She generously doled out compliments and thought every single man in the room was checking out whichever one of us was feeling lousy that day.

"More like Pretty Woman," Isla said, pushing her glasses up her nose. "And I don't mean in the sense that they got together in the end. I mean in the way that he's a prick who thinks he can buy a woman."

"Shh, shh," Savannah said, waving her hand. "You cannot shit on Pretty Woman. I won't listen. I love that movie!"

"She has no value until she meets him. That's the message of the movie."

That was Isla. She didn't believe in romance. She was jaded from dating apps, where she only seemed to attract the most patronizing men on the planet. Ironic, given Isla was never going to do anything other than speak her mind.

She was the friend who had told a director to go fuck himself when he'd suggested she wasn't feminine enough and who had gone after a guy in a bar who would not stop harassing us while dancing. Baseball-hat-sideways-guy had put his hand on Savannah's butt and that had been the end of his fun. Isla had his arm behind his back in two seconds while he protested in pain and she asked him if he liked being touched without his permission.

Isla had left the cutthroat entertainment industry for the equally cutthroat restaurant business and was thriving there.

Savannah covered her ears. "I told you, I'm not listening!"

"They'll do this all night," Dakota said. "So ignore them and tell us how it felt to play a rich man's girlfriend for the day."

Amazing. Though there was no way in hell I was admitting that out loud. I decided to focus on the oddities of it. "Grant had very specific ideas about what he wanted me to wear, so that was weird. But otherwise, the opportunity to put on designer clothes was fantastic."

"Do you get to keep them?" Felicia asked. "Is that in the contract?"

I stared blankly at her for a second. "I never thought to ask. I don't know. I mean, maybe? It's not like he can return them." My brain hadn't gone that far forward. "But I have to treat this the same way as a costume. That's what it is—a costume to get in character."

Hey, we all tell ourselves lies.

I was just including my friends in my attempt to lie to myself.

"Method acting. Sure." Felicia nodded. "But if he can't return them, make sure you ask for the clothes. You can sell them for gobs of money."

The thought of selling such beautiful garments was like having a bouquet of fresh blooms ripped out of my hands and tossed onto the ground, but she was right. It was the practical thing to do. Maybe I could sell certain pieces and keep others.

Sure, to wear to Duane Reade to buy shampoo. I mentally eyerolled myself. I didn't have a designer life.

Felicia was the practical one of our bunch, and the queen of the hustle. She could make money appear like the internet was her personal sofa cushion. She just lifted and loose change was there, mingling with crumbs and hair. She scoured online auctions and real-life thrift shops and turned around and resold them for a profit. It was a time-consuming occupation but she seemed to revel in it. She'd once described it akin to gambling, the thrill of watching numbers.

"I will never do that," I said. "You know me. They'll be in my closet for years before I have the ambition to put them online."

"I'll do it for you for a ten percent commission."

"Sold." When I thought about what the clothes had cost it was kind of staggering to think I could wind up with thousands more from this job. Besides, we lived in the same apartment so I could just walk the clothes four feet to Felicia's room.

"That's so gross," Savannah complained. "Those were *gifts*. You can't sell gifts."

Felicia, who was more up on the latest fashion trends and designers was on her phone. "I'm looking at Chanel's social media. Are any of these pieces what you got?" She started to turn the screen for me to see, then said, "Oh my God, Leah, this is you! On this woman's page. She tagged you. I think she's a sales consultant."

"What? Let me see!"

We all jumped off our stools and huddled around her, staring at the screen over Felicia's shoulder. "It's me singing," I said, stunned. "I knew she was recording and she asked if she could post it, but I didn't actually think she would."

"You sound fantastic," Dakota said. "You don't sing as often as you should."

I gave her a look. Sometimes the obvious eluded Dakota. "Are you kidding me? I sing at work every day, you just don't see it."

"Oh, right." Dakota laughed.

Felicia played it again. "Look at how many views, Leah. A couple thousand. That's awesome."

"My fifteen seconds of fame. Literally." I was proud of the way I sounded without any sort of warmup. The designer outfit made me look different than I did in real life. My expression was serene, the mirror to the sides of me casting an intriguing reflective light over the whole scene. It felt staged instead of spontaneous.

"She tagged Grant too."

I wasn't sure how I felt about that. It would serve his purpose to let it be known we were together, but did I really want the world at large to think we were a couple? What would that mean for my personal life? Especially given that it wasn't even true. "That seems presumptuous of her."

"Why? You're 'dating.'" Isla made air quotes. "It seems natural she would tag him too. Especially given he was footing the bill for the clothes. Does it matter?"

No. "It doesn't. I don't know. Sorry, I don't mean to be weird."

Fortunately for me, Savannah changed the subject when she spotted a guy. "Oh my God, Isla, that guy is totally checking you out. Don't look."

Isla, predictably, turned around with zero subtlety. "That guy? He's wearing a wedding ring."

"Oh, never mind. Wait. Unless he's a widow and he's still healing from his loss. I mean, that's a tricky issue. When do you take the ring off?" Savannah gazed thoughtfully at the man who was wearing far too predatory a look to be a grieving widow.

"The amazing thing is, she's serious," Dakota said.

"Do you think statistically the number of widows is higher than cheating men?" Isla asked. "Because I don't. I think it's like ten thousand to one."

We were in a bar that had popped up in the East Village a few months earlier. It was close to the theater and catered more to New Yorkers in service than the rich or famous. Or even tourists. It wasn't what I would call a dive, but it was tucked away and the prices were reasonable. We'd been a few times and we'd liked the atmosphere because it wasn't one of pickups and general douchery.

"Look," Felicia said, showing me her phone again. "I found your boss online."

I was surprised to see that Grant had a social media account though I wasn't sure why that surprised me. I reached out and scrolled through the posts. They were rare and were usually alcohol or vacation vistas. Several shots of him with gorgeous women on his arm. He always looked mildly irritated. "Wait, these are just times he was tagged, right? He's never actually posted."

"It looks like he had an account and he deleted it. But yes, these are tags. Oh, look, there's a story with him in it right now." She tapped and we saw Grant at a bar, leaning on the counter, his arm around a woman who weighed three pounds and had blonde extensions that went to her ass. She somehow managed to be kissing his cheek, while simultaneously looking at the camera. "Who is that?" Felicia asked.

"I don't know," I said, as jealousy stabbed me in the gut like Satan's pitchfork. "Seems kind of stupid to pay me all this money to be his girlfriend when he's running around with Miss Blonde Isn't My Natural Color."

Dakota made a cat meowing sound. "Settle down, geez. It's not exactly a crime to dye your hair and he's just your boss. Remember?"

The story disappeared when Felicia let go of the image and I sipped my wine, a lump in my throat. "You're right," I said, even though inside I was picturing murdering Dakota for her insufferable logic. Nothing was logical when you had a crush, even at the age of twenty-six.

And I did have a crush. I'd maintained that all along and it wasn't going away. If anything, it was getting worse because Grant looked sexy as hell, kissed like a savant, and got me slippers.

Slippers I was still wearing, which had mortified Felicia, but whatever. My ankle hurt like a motherfucker. Too much pretend runway walking.

Trying to keep my phone under the table so no one could see what I was doing, I texted Grant.

No one is going to believe I'm your girlfriend if you are out with other women.

I hovered over the up arrow and then changed my mind. I couldn't send that. It sounded bitchy. It was none of my business. Besides, he would know I looked him up on social media and that was embarrassing. Though I could claim it was for research purposes, to better prepare for my role as fake girlfriend.

Still. The text sounded bitchy.

I used the back arrow to start deleting what I had typed.

"What are you doing?" Isla asked. She reached over Dakota and grabbed my phone. "No one texts under the table unless they're being shady and we're all sitting here so you are not texting any of us. That leaves only one likely person you could be texting."

"Okay, Detective Parker, yes, I am texting Grant. But I changed my mind," I said, feeling grumpy about the whole thing. Obviously, Grant hadn't enjoyed our day together as much as I had if he was out with another woman. "I started to delete it."

"I'm deleting the rest of it." She tapped on my phone. "And I'm keeping your phone."

"No, you're not. I swear I won't text him." Unless he texted me first.

Isla put my phone in her bra.

"That's stealing," I told her. "And I will dig in your bra to get it back." I stood up so I could get closer to Isla.

She laughed and tossed my phone back on the table. "As much as I'd love to have you feel my boob, here. I didn't know it was that important to you."

"You're wearing the bracelet he gave you!" Dakota said, with her usual booming voice. She could knock pigeons out of nests with her pitch. She also pointed to my wrist, just in case anyone in the tri-state area had missed what she meant.

I winced. I was wearing the bracelet. "I'm a mermaid in the show. The bracelet is sparkly. It seemed fitting."

"Oh, sweetie," Savannah said, rubbing her hand over mine.

"You're in love with your boss. That never ends well."

That sobered me up. "I'm not in love with him. Relax. I barely know him. But yes, fine, I like Grant. I've never denied that."

"He texted you," Felicia said. "It says, 'Can you talk later? How did the show go?'"

"Can you not read my texts!" I said, snatching my phone off the table. "I thought we were here to celebrate my show, not troll me."

"We're just teasing you," Isla said. "Sorry, Leah. I didn't know it would upset you that much."

I actually felt like my cheeks were burning. Grant Caldwell made me blush, oh my God, how ridiculous.

I texted Grant back.

Out with friends but I should be home soon. Are you at home? The show went great, thanks!

There. That was casual, right?

Out with my cousin Victoria and her boyfriend but I'll be home soon too.

The relief I felt that the blonde was his cousin was inappropriate and embarrassing and I would walk over a path of burning Legos before I would admit it out loud.

Now what? I didn't want to sound too eager to talk to him.

So I took a picture of my feet with the slippers on and held my wine glass in front of them. I sent it to Grant.

That's my girl.

His response went straight to my inner thighs.

So much so that I slapped my phone down on the table and

took a sip of wine, hoping to cool myself down. It didn't work.

I realized no one was speaking. All four of my friends were staring at me with various expressions. Isla looked thoughtful. Savannah looked hopeful. Felicia worried. Dakota amused. "What?" I asked defensively.

"I just want to remember this moment," Savannah said. "This is the day your destiny changed. I just know it."

Why did I feel this tiny seed of panic that she might be right? That this job might have consequences I couldn't even fathom at this point. That I mentally checked myself. Like what? A newfound appreciation for slippers? An obsession with maple syrup?

It might spoil me a little with the awesome clothes and the excellent kissing, but the only life-changing aspect would be the seriously fat paycheck.

"This is like the movie Serendipity," Savannah said.

"It's not even close to that," Isla protested.

"Let me have my rom-coms!" Savannah said, her voice rising dramatically.

I was taking a sip of wine when she said that and it was so over-the-top I choked on my wine from laughter. "Isla is a dream crusher. Don't worry, Savannah. I believe heavily in the rom-com. After all, Overboard is what brought me and Grant together."

"Oooh, you said *together*!" Savannah pointed a finger at me.

"That's not what I meant! You know what I meant! It brought me to this job. That's what I meant."

I was over explaining and over protesting.

Overboard. That's what I was.

I drained the rest of my wine and reminded myself I was an actress.

This was a role. Don't confuse art with reality.

The server came by. "Another glass of wine."

I nodded emphatically.

Bourbon, bacon, and Bali. Your turn.

Bacardi, bread, and Buffalo.

That made me laugh. Of course Leah would say Buffalo. She had started texting me at night with three "favorites" with a random letter and then I would respond in kind. It was part of getting to know me, she'd said.

It was mostly a game, a glimpse into her sense of humor.

But yes, we were learning about each other.

Tonight she hadn't texted me yet, so I had started the thread because it amused me. She amused me.

So it was favorite cocktail, food, and place.

I had just entered my apartment and was in the kitchen, chopping up some vegetables to throw in a stir-fry. I don't love to cook but sometimes it's just easier than constantly ordering takeout or wasting a couple of hours in a restaurant. We were leaving for my parents' house in the morning and I had a lot to do, including packing. My living room was filled with the packages of clothing for Leah and her new set of luggage.

The dreaded trip that had felt like punishment now was something I was looking forward to. I both felt like I was besting my father and getting to spend time with Leah.

Whiskey, waffles, Warsaw.

Washington apple, walnuts, Westminster. W is hard. Pick a better letter. And you don't like waffles.

I popped a raw sliced pepper into my mouth. *Water chestnuts.*

Really? No one likes those.

And no one lives in Buffalo.

I knew that would annoy her. I was kidding of course. I didn't really believe Buffalo was a myth. It just was bizarre to me that in all my years in business I had never actually met someone who was from Buffalo. Leah was the first.

Point made. Buffalo has a population of 248,000 people. Maybe one or two like water chestnuts.

I wanted to use the letter L but I was struggling to come up with an L cocktail I actually liked. I decided it didn't matter if that one was a stretching of the truth.

Long Island Iced Tea, lentils, Leah's bed.

Haha. Cute.

Lemon Drop, lasagna, Los Angeles.

I was going to hand her an opening and I hoped she would take it.

Gin, garbanzo beans, Geneva.

Grasshopper (not really, but I can't think of another G drink), guacamole, Grant's pants.

I laughed. She came through exactly the way I wanted her to.

So come and watch me eat water chestnuts. You can eat the rest of the stir-fry and then get in my pants.

I sent her a picture of the cutting board with all the vegetables laid out.

We're supposed to leave tomorrow. That seems like a lot of back and forth for me.

Bring your toiletries bag and spend the night. We can leave from here.

There was a bubble on my phone like she was typing. It disappeared and no text was sent. She was clearly thinking. Probably how to politely tell me to fuck off.

I texted her again.

Sazerac, stir-fry, sex?

I thought this weekend was supposed to be sex free.

It's not the weekend yet.

Sangria, stir-fry, sex.

I'm not going to say I did a fist pump but I'm not going to say I didn't do a fist pump.

I was used to getting what I wanted but this felt like a serious win. I wanted Leah in my bed. I wanted to taste her skin and sink inside her body.

White or red wine? I can send a car for you.

Red. I can take the train. What's your address?

I sent her the information and then looked around my kitchen. Time to double up the serving size and whip up some sangria. I went into my room and changed out of my suit and into a pair of jeans and a T-shirt.

By the time I had the sangria made and more vegetables ready to hit the wok, Leah texted.

I'm in the lobby.

I'll be right down.

Just tell me what floor.

I want to come down and get you.

Leah called me on FaceTime. "Why?" she asked the second her face appeared. "It will be faster if I just come up."

I went to my front door and opened it as I talked to her. "Because I'm a fucking gentleman," I told her mildly.

After stepping into my sandals I kept in the foyer to my apartment, I walked into the hallway and closed my door behind me but didn't lock it. It was a safe building.

Leah raised her eyebrows. "You're a true romantic, Grant Caldwell. The third."

Hardly. "No one has ever accused me of that, but I do like to think I have manners. I'm getting on the elevator now. I'll see you in a minute."

When I got downstairs Leah was standing there in leggings, an oversized sweatshirt, and the purple slippers. There was a backpack slung over her shoulder. She looked like she had wandered down the hall of her dorm to talk to a friend.

"Hi," I said, kissing her impulsively and taking her backpack. "Let me carry that for you. Thanks for coming over."

"This is what you get on short notice," she said, gesturing to her outfit.

Her hair was on her head in a messy bun. I didn't mind. This casual look was more reminiscent of the way she looked at the diner. "You always look beautiful. And very kissable."

"Just a warning. I'm keeping these slippers on all night." She gave me a grin. "For everything."

"You can wear whatever you want on your feet as long as you're naked everywhere else." I hit the elevator up button.

"If you can keep a straight face while these fuzzy slippers are propped on your shoulders, I am going to be very impressed with your focus."

I raised my eyebrows as the elevator door opened. The thought of her legs spread up on either side of me made my cock hard and my mouth water. I wasn't going to give a shit what she was encasing her feet in at that point. "Challenge accepted. My focus is legendary."

"For sure. I've seen you eat pancakes." Leah made a stabbing gesture as we stepped into the elevator that was more Psycho shower scene than breakfast consumption.

"I don't do that," I protested. "You can't just fork it."

"You do."

"I do not."

"This is a ridiculous conversation."

"You started it."

"I don't think that I did, actually," I told her. "But I'm willing to change the subject. That's a small backpack. Do you have everything in there you need for the weekend?" The door opened on my floor and I put my arm across it so Leah could exit first.

"I hope so. I have toiletries, makeup, a bra for that cocktail dress, and three thongs."

"No pajamas?" If she intended to sleep naked, that was both

amazing and brutal. But I'd made a promise not to touch her. I opened my apartment door for her.

She gestured to her current outfit. "I can sleep in this."

That was fucking disappointing. "You're going to get hot in that sweatshirt."

"Nah. I don't sweat." She looked around my living room. "Oh my God, is this the clothes you got for me to wear? It's like twenty-five boxes!"

"It's just a lot of tissue and packing materials. After we eat, we can put everything into your luggage." I eyed her backpack again. "Did you pack shoes? I know you're in a committed relationship with your slippers right now, but I would prefer you not wear them all weekend." I couldn't even picture how much attention she would receive—and none of it good—if she shuffled around the Hamptons in slippers.

"I brought one pair of ballet flats."

I eyed her ankle as I closed my door and kicked off my sandals. "How is your sprain?" I could make a phone call and get her some heels for the actual anniversary party. It had been ten days and I didn't want her to reinjure herself, but we needed a slipper alternative.

"It's fine."

I didn't believe her. She looked like she was trying to say what I wanted to hear. I decided I would get some sneakers and she could go for a very cool and young Rihanna kind of look, with a sexy dress and Kicks. I set her backpack down on my sofa.

"Are you hungry now?" I asked as I went and poured her a

glass of sangria. It wasn't my best work, but it was short notice sangria. I handed it to her.

Leah took a sip and said, "I'm starving. Let's do this thing. How can I help? Though I have to warn you I never cook. You saw my kitchen. We pretty much have an Easy Bake oven."

"I'm not a great cook either but this is just vegetables in a wok. We can't screw it up."

"You underestimate my ability to screw things up." Leah gave me a grin. She sipped her sangria.

I made myself a Sazerac because that's what I had said in my text. I had a decent at-home bar because while I don't usually have more than one drink, I wanted the option of being able to make whatever I was in the mood for.

"This is a nice apartment," Leah said. "Your kitchen is amazing."

"Thanks. I've been happy with it. It's the open concept I like."

Leah leaned on the island and watched me. "What is that?"

"A Sazerac."

Understanding dawned on her. "Of course. What's in it?" She reached for one of the bottles I had set down.

"Rye. Bitters. Sugar. Lemon. Absinthe on the rim if you have it, which I don't."

"Can I taste it?"

"As my fake girlfriend, whatever's mine is yours."

"I think that applies to spouses only."

I handed her my mixed drink. "Maybe we'll have to upgrade our status." That would get my parents off my ass for years. In the meantime, I could take measures to secure my position at the company and make sure my father's stipulations were null and void.

Leah choked on the Sazerac. "Are you serious? Grant. Marriage isn't something to joke about or fake. It's a serious commitment."

I shrugged. "Not to my parents. They've made their own rules up as they went."

She studied me. "That doesn't mean you have to behave the same way as them."

"I haven't. That's why I'm not married. I don't make promises I can't keep." I was a lot of things—workaholic, aggressive, confident—but I wasn't dishonest.

Leah nodded, slowly, like she wasn't sure of what to make of my response. "If you're going to fake propose to me, just give me a warning." She handed me the Sazerac back. "Now let's get cooking. I'm starving."

She came around the other side of the island to join me at the stove. I realized I had never had a woman in my kitchen with me. The rye was sliding smoothly down my throat and I suddenly felt tense, aware. All these questions, all these moments with Leah, had been fun, flirtatious. She amused me and turned me on.

But the way she had looked at me just now—like she didn't approve of me—didn't sit well. I wanted her to like me.

Holy fuck. I wanted her to like me because I liked her.

Emotions were rising to the surface that surprised me and it wasn't a comfortable feeling. It was like being out sailing and a sudden storm pops up and shoves you off course. And tosses icy ocean water all over your face.

So I did what I'd been doing since I was a kid. Ignore the fuck out of them.

I picked up a water chestnut and held it up to Leah. "Sure you don't want to try one of these beauties? They're good plain. Amazing soaked in soy sauce."

"Get that away from me." Leah grabbed my wrist and moved my arm out of range of her mouth.

"You should try new things."

"I've tried them. It's like biting into frozen grass. That sound." She shuddered. "It's a nightmare."

I popped it into my mouth and ate it. "I don't hear anything."

"I'll have a pepper." She picked a slice off the cutting board and lifted it to her lips.

Then she flicked her tongue over it. "Mmm. Red peppers are delicious."

She might be fucking with me, but she was damn sexy doing it. I took another sip of my drink. "You seem to be passionate about them."

"I am." She sucked the pepper slice. "So much flavor. Do you want to taste?"

She may be talking about vegetables but I had different ideas in mind. The stir-fry could wait. "I'd love a taste."

Leah held up the pepper.

I bit the end off. Then I drew her fingertip into my mouth and sucked.

Her eyes darkened.

"What vegetable are you passionate about?" she asked, her

voice low, gaze drifting to watch me suck her finger before I bit the tip gently and let her go.

"I save my passions for my bedroom."

"Just your bedroom?" she asked, reaching for another slice of pepper.

I took the cutting board and shifted it to my stovetop, though she did manage to snag one more pepper piece. I took both of our glasses and moved them off of the island to the expanse of countertop next to the stove. Turning back to her, I put my hands on her waist and set her ass down on the marble.

"No. My passions are on full display anywhere I'm with you."

Then I kissed her, hand slipping under her sweatshirt to discover that she had on no bra. I palmed her nipple and dipped my tongue inside her mouth, wanting her. Now. It had been ten days and every night I'd gone to sleep thinking about how she had tasted.

I stepped back and pulled her sweatshirt off over her head.

"I thought we were eating first," she said, leaning back on the palms of her hands so that tits thrust forward in open, mouthwatering invitation. "Sazerac, stir-fry, sex. That's what you said."

"That wasn't indicative of order, just desire and intent." I shifted my hand down into her leggings and teased over her clit. "It wasn't legal and binding."

"Don't corporate talk me," Leah said.

Damn. I undid my pants. "How about I just fuck you?"

"I wouldn't hate that," she said.

CHAPTER 8

So obviously, I knew what I was getting into when I agreed to come over to Grant's. Or rather, what was getting into *me*.

But Grant was so different from the other men I had been with and in the best way possible. He purposely dropped lines he knew would catch me off guard. I wondered if we were together, together, in the way that Savannah had thought I was saying, how far he would go with the alpha aggression.

Way further than now, because there would be trust.

And I would love it.

But we wouldn't be together, together, so I was just going to enjoy every minute he was touching me.

Right then he was stroking me to full and complete arousal while kissing me like we were on a plane that was going down. Desperate. Passionate. With everything. I'd never been kissed the way Grant did. It was all his usual control shattered when our lips touched and he unleashed the darkest most reckless parts of himself onto me.

Our passion was like wildfire. It sparked, grew, then ran wild across the landscape, leaving everything in its path searing hot.

It was overwhelming in the best way possible. I gripped his shoulders and spread my knees further as he nudged between my legs, into my space. My feet went slack and my slippers dropped to the floor from gravity.

"Lie down," he said, pulling his hand out of my leggings, leaving me aching with desire.

"What?" I couldn't even picture how that would work. But I obeyed and instantly regretted it. "Yikes, that's cold." Even though my skin was flushed with desire, it was a brutal shock.

I was about to shoot back off but Grant was yanking my legging off. Before I could even process what was happening, he had me off the cold stone and in his arms. I grabbed his biceps, needing somewhere to hold on. Grant turned us both and pushed me against the nearest wall. Wanting to feel his skin on mine, I yanked up the bottom of his T-shirt.

With a skill reminiscent of Houdini, he had a condom out of his pocket, his pants down, and all that gorgeous hot cock covered in latex. It was a thing of wonder and delight. Both the movement and his cock. In the ten days since we'd had sex, I'd convinced myself I had exaggerated the length. The girth. The skill.

That after my Halloween debacle of the year before, I'd been so hungry to believe in the existence of good sex, I had turned Grant into a savant when maybe he wasn't.

All of that was wrong.

I hadn't exaggerated a damn thing and he was a savant.

He was a sexual unicorn in my world.

Something I had always hoped existed but had thought was most likely a fantasy.

He might not sparkle but he fucked like a rock star.

I was holding on, head thrown back, making sounds I hadn't even known I was capable of, as he held me like I weighed nothing and thrust up inside me. Grant kissed me again, and the warm wet tease of his tongue over mine mimicked the deep slide of his cock into me. My orgasm showed up without warning and for a split second I couldn't breathe. Or think. Or move.

I just locked eyes with Grant and felt the most intense pleasure I'd experienced in years. Maybe ever.

It was deep and powerful and desperate.

Grant's grip on my ass was firm, and after I murmured, "Oh, God," my orgasm finally fading, he yanked me up higher.

I had been slipping and hadn't realized it.

"You feel so fucking amazing," he said.

I was starting to wonder if it was an "us" thing because for a man who had most likely been around the block a few, or ten thousand times, was either by nature over-the-top complimentary (doubtful) or we had chemistry.

Just good old-fashioned, no-explanation-for-it, sexual chemistry.

Grant came with a low growl, his forehead pressed against mine.

He pulled back and shook his head a little. "Damn, you make me lose control."

"That's kind of the point," I told him, easing my grip on his arms. "Isn't it?"

"I've never thought about it that way. I thought the point was pleasure." Grant eased out of me and set me carefully down on the floor. He rubbed his beard, a gesture I'd noticed he took to when he was contemplative.

I was totally naked while he was mostly dressed but it didn't bother me. I was comfortable in my skin and didn't feel any need to hide. I took the few steps to where my sangria was and took a sip. "Where's your bathroom?"

"First door down on the right." He pointed to the hallway as he removed the condom and tossed it under the sink. He started washing his hands. "Unless you want to take a shower. Then you can go to my bedroom at the end of the hall."

"No. I'm starving." I just wanted to pee. I bent over and scooped up my pile of clothes he'd discarded.

Grant made a sound and I sensed him moving toward me. I laughed and darted out of his reach. "No! No seconds right now."

He groaned. "You're cruel."

To which I stopped, turned, and gave him a faux scathing look. "Grant. Twice now I've had sex with you within ten minutes of us being in a private place. If that's cruel, I can't even fathom what kind is."

Grant smiled. "I can't argue with that. But you can't blame me for wanting more. We have great chemistry."

Confirmation of my thoughts. He knew it just as clearly as I did. "We do." I pointed to the stove. "Now cook us a meal and we'll see what happens afterwards. We have all night."

Our only night. We weren't having sex at his parents' house, something we both felt strongly about for different reasons. We had to make this night count.

His powder room was what I would have expected. Modern, shiny finishes. Very clean, tidy. I was sure he had a cleaning lady because the image of Grant with a toilet brush in his hand was too hilarious for words. I wasn't wowed by expensive possessions but at the same time I couldn't help but run my hands over the walnut vanity and take extra time drying my hands off on towels so plush they might have been a comforter. I redid my topknot as I glanced around, trying to see if I could learn anything about Grant. But it was just a guest powder room and it appeared sterile.

I put my panties and sweatshirt on but skipped the leggings. Getting in and out of them was like filling a piping bag. You just kept cramming until suddenly they were filled. How they could be so comfortable once on your body and yet such a bitch to get into was one of the wonders of the world. Given that I was intending for Grant to want them off again (and likewise) I decided to save him the trouble. I did want my slippers back on though.

When I returned to the kitchen and bent over to pick up my slippers and slide them onto my feet, Grant was stirring the vegetables in the wok.

"You forgot your pants," he said.

"I'm taking a shortcut. Saving you some trouble later."

"That's very thoughtful."

"I'm just drawn that way." I padded over to him. "What's going on here? How can I help?"

"I think I've got it." Grant turned and pulled me against his chest. He had a bemused expression on his face.

He looked relaxed. Not so intense. Not so controlled. Just in his element. Content.

I was feeling things I shouldn't be feeling. Curiosity. Tenderness. Attraction that included lust but also went beyond it. I wrapped my arms around his waist and studied him.

"What?" he asked. "Are you wondering how it's possible I'm this good looking?"

I rolled my eyes. "I'm trying to picture you without a beard."

"I look like a naked mole rat."

That made me laugh. "Good visual. Pink skin. I'm properly horrified."

"We can't have that." Grant bent down and cupped my cheeks. He kissed with the same fervor as before, as if he couldn't get enough.

It took me right back to desperate need and we moved our bodies closer, tongues teasing at each other. Grant's hand shifted to my ass and he rocked me forward in a soft rhythm that had me brushing against him. My head drifted back and he kissed my neck, his beard scratching my tender flesh.

Then I realized that the vegetables were burning. Smoke was rising behind his head and the distinct odor hit my nostrils. "Grant, dinner is burning." I patted his arm to get him to release me.

He didn't react as quickly as I would have expected. He looked back and just slowly turned the burner off. He waved his hand half-heartedly in the air.

I had a thought. "Turn your fan on. The clothes you got me are going to smell like burned oil." The boxes were fifteen feet away but I could already see the smoke was rising and circling around his ceiling.

"Shit." That lit a fire under his butt. He turned the fan on and quickly walked over to his living room windows. "These only open about six inches for safety reasons but it should help."

I looked around for a blanket. I felt like I needed to save the clothes. Cover them from stinky smoke. I didn't see anything I could use to save the Chanel. "If I had a window, which I don't, there would be no safety restrictions. My roommates' windows lift like four feet and Javier's has a fire escape he uses to climb out onto and smoke weed."

"Javier? Your roommate is a guy?" Grant was waving his arms like somehow he could draw the smoke to the windows.

"Yes." I took the wok by the handle and dumped the still smoking vegetables into the stainless steel can in the corner of the kitchen. It had a foot pedal and the lid slammed shut tightly, sealing it off. "I think we're clear." The smoke seemed to be dissipating.

"Does your roommate have a girlfriend? Boyfriend?" he asked, clearly fishing for information.

"No." I wasn't going to give him any further information than that. Javier and I were strictly platonic friends and if he specifically wanted to know that, he could just ask. Though it did give me a warm sensation in inappropriate places that he looked put out by potential competition. "I guess we need to order food. Have I mentioned I'm starving?"

"This is the third time so I guess I need to take you seriously. What kind of food do you want?"

"Somewhere we can get guacamole. I'm even more passionate about guac than I am peppers." I dropped the wok in Grant's sink and tried to figure out how to turn the faucet on. I didn't see any handles or knobs. "Um, how does this work?"

"Wave your hands under it or tap the side."

I did and water hit the wok. It made me feel like I was in a public restroom but I suppose it was more sanitary than faucets. "Order food and I'll start packing while we're waiting."

"That's a good plan." Grant was on his phone, scrolling.

I washed my hands so they would be clean for the very expensive clothes and went into the living room. I set a suitcase on its side and opened it. Not surprisingly, it was the highest quality suitcase I'd ever seen. I opened several boxes inside bags and various garments were wrapped in tissue. Some were items I didn't even recognize, like a pair of jeans and a chunky sweater. I found delicate earrings and statement necklaces. One necklace was so elaborate and gorgeous, an emerald and gold piece of artwork that I had to try it on. I clasped it around my neck and found a mirror above a console table by the entryway.

The purity of its beauty was being lost in the dingy gray of my sweatshirt. So I took it off and checked it out again. "This necklace is so beautiful, Grant. Did you pick it out?" I turned a little, admiring the shimmer.

"What necklace?" Grant said, coming up behind me and running his hands down my arms. "All I see is an almost naked you."

And he said he wasn't romantic.

I lifted my gaze from the stunning necklace to watch Grant as he eased his large hands over my sides, and onto my breasts. He wasn't looking at me in the mirror. He was staring down at my shoulders before he dropped his head and kissed my bare skin. It gave me goose bumps. It felt like more than he intended. It felt real. It felt seductive. It felt beyond sex.

It both made me shiver in delight and want to run. I couldn't do this. I could not be the idiot who fell for the man who insisted he didn't do relationships. I couldn't have predicted how the last guy I'd dated had turned out (hello, can't hold his liquor), but Grant was predictable. Javier had said as much. He ran through women at a high percentage rate.

The necklace sparkled and reflected back at me as Grant teased at my nipples and I looked exactly like what I was—a woman falling for a man who was all wrong for her.

I should run like a serial killer with a raised ax was chasing me.

I didn't, obviously.

Nope. Not even so much as a step away from him. I just closed my eyes and let myself get swept away in the moment.

That's how I needed to treat being with Grant. I had to just enjoy each moment in and of itself and not worry about what it was, or really, what it wasn't.

He was coaxing me to a slow easy orgasm, his hand inside my panties, when a loud squawk made me jump. "What the hell?"

Grant stepped back and gave a casual shrug, like he hadn't just abandoned me three seconds from satisfaction. "I think that's the front door buzzer for our dinner. You're starving, remember?"

"That was ridiculously efficient," I complained.

"I'll leave a bad review." Grant opened his door just a sliver so he could squeeze through without anyone seeing me. "Be right back."

With a sigh I dragged my sweatshirt back on over my head and removed the necklace. I knew myself well enough to know I just might drop guacamole on my chest at some point. It probably wasn't easy to get mashed avocado out of intricate jewelry.

When Grant came back into the apartment, I took the bag from him. "I need to eat my feelings."

His eyebrows shot up. "What feelings are those?"

I opened the bag and popped a chip into my mouth. "Hunger and sexual frustration."

"I can take care of both of those."

I had no doubt.

Eating with Leah was the first time it occurred to me I didn't have a table. I ate at the island, on the sofa, or at my desk. There was room for a dining table, I'd just never gotten one because it seemed unnecessary. I didn't even remember the designer suggesting one, now that I thought about it. Maybe I threw off a vibe of workaholic dude eats alone or in restaurants.

But while eating at the island next to Leah felt casual and comfortable, it would have been better to be able to sit across from her and see her as we talked. A real meal at a table in my own apartment with a woman. It had never mattered to me. But with Leah the idea held appeal.

Everything about Leah held appeal.

She had destroyed a burrito in about thirty seconds and was now eating plantain chips with guacamole while firing questions at me with a speed of three per minute. Or close to it.

"Sunrises or sunsets?"

"Sunset. I love the night. Besides, the sunset is when you applaud yourself for an accomplished day."

"I'm the opposite," she said. "I love the possibilities of a new day."

That didn't surprise me about Leah. She was a very optimistic person.

"What's your favorite dessert?" she asked.

"You," I said without hesitation.

Leah laughed. "No, I meant for real. I love key lime pie. I would do some shady things for a slice of it."

"I'll make note of that." Seriously, I was going to have to send her a whole key lime pie next week as a thank-you gift. No vibrator included. Just the pie. "That's good ammunition to have."

She rolled her eyes. "What's your answer?"

I thought about it and shrugged. "I don't know. I'm not a big dessert guy. I guess maybe chocolate cake."

"Solid choice." Leah stuck her finger in the guacamole container and scraped the last remaining bits up. "Do you speak another language?"

The random questions kept coming. "Yes. French, learned at boarding school. Spanish, taught to me by my nanny. How about you?"

"Nope. I suck. I really should learn Spanish at least but I don't seem to have an ear for it."

"It's not an ear. It's not intellect. You have to *feel* a language."

"Interesting. Not what I would have expected you to say."

"I do know how to feel things."

Leah grinned. "I know you do."

I nodded. "And I'm just getting started."

"I can't wait to see what you mean by that." But then she went right back to drilling me. "How long have you lived here?" she asked.

"Two years."

"Rent or own?"

"Rent. I realize that's ironic given I own real estate but I have a penthouse in mind that is eighteen months out from completion. I moved in here intending it to be temporary but then I couldn't find the right property." The place I wanted was insanely huge for a single guy but it seemed like the next logical step.

"I've never been in an actual penthouse. I have a friend who has access to a communal rooftop deck and that seemed amazing enough. When I picture a penthouse, I am imagining a private elevator and a giant glass box where you stand at the corner and stare down onto Manhattan with your hands behind your back while curtains mysteriously blow even though the windows don't open."

That amused me. "That's a very specific visual. I bet I could do that here." I set down my own burrito and went to the windows, which were still open from burning the stir-fry. I spread my legs, stared out the window and put my hands behind my back. "I'm the King of Manhattan," I said. "Everything I see I own."

"You're an idiot."

Leave it to Leah to refuse to enjoy my bad acting. I stared her down over my shoulder. "Only my mother is allowed to speak to me like that. You will be punished."

"I'm really scared," she said cheerfully.

"I can see that." I went back to the island and invaded her personal space with my body.

Leah paused with a chip halfway to her mouth. I took the chip and ate it.

"Hey." But she sounded more turned on than pissed off. "That was mine."

"I'll order you more chips if you want. But right now, you're going to answer a question for *me*."

"Is this you being Robert De Niro or someone similar or are you being yourself?"

"I'm being me." I spun her stool so she was facing me and I rested my palms on her bare knees. I had her boxed in and I could hear her breathing deepen in arousal.

Everything about her drove me crazy. Even now, as she dragged her tongue over her bottom lip to moisten it, and stared up at me defiantly, I thought she was the hottest thing I'd ever seen.

I wanted to ask her why she didn't have a boyfriend. There had to be thousands of men in New York who would love to spend their days and nights with her. She was a ray of sunshine with a hefty side of sexy. But asking that would never sound anything less than rude as fuck and I wasn't that stupid. I also wanted to ask her why she wasn't a star, because that too seemed like a mystery. But if she knew why she wasn't a star, presumably she'd change it and be a star. So again, another question that would just annoy her.

So I asked what I still didn't have total confirmation on. "Were you really flirting with me at the diner or just screwing with me?"

"That's an easy question. I thought you were going to ask something difficult. Yes, I was flirting with you. But my skills as a temptress in real life are not renowned." Leah put her hands on my arms. "Why does it matter?"

"I'm trying to figure out actress you versus real you."

"Maybe I prefer to keep you guessing."

I didn't like that answer. I decided to take control. I scooped her up off the stool. "I know one thing you aren't faking."

"Prove it." She wrapped her arms around my neck and gave me a challenging smile.

"Game on." I took Leah into my bedroom and set her down on the bed.

She looked good there. All dark hair and naughty smile. The sweatshirt was so oversized, her lean legs descending below the bulk, her fingers wrapped around the sleeve cuffs, it looked like it could be my shirt. Something about that concept made me feel turned on and male and dominant. Territorial. I liked the look of her in my bed.

I took my shirt off and tossed it in the direction of my bathroom.

She was looking around the room. "Very nice. Like a hotel. You're very tidy."

"I like order." I undid my pants and was getting on the bed when she put her hand on my chest. "Yes?" I asked. She didn't look like she planned to stop me. But more like she had a request.

"What's your view like? Is it private? Or is it like the living room? I'd love to see the city view."

Given that she didn't have a window at all in her bedroom, it seemed like a reasonable request. "It's a similar view. I'll open the blinds." I had a remote control so I reached over her and picked it up off the nightstand and hit the correct buttons.

"Now that's handy," Leah said. "I like it."

"You take in the view." I tugged her sweatshirt up over her breasts. She was on her back, gazing at the windows. "I'm going to take you."

"Deal."

That made me laugh under my breath. It was such a Leah response.

And that thought gave me pause. A Leah response. I knew that because I was getting to know her. I realized I had devoted more time to talking to her in ten days than I had with women I had dated for two months. I couldn't predict what Leah would say yet, or finish her sentences, but I had a pretty damn good idea of how her mind worked and what made her tick.

She found awe in almost everything. Or if not pure awe, at least amusement or fascination or *something*. She liked to have conversations like a tennis match. Volley. Back and forth.

Right now, she was studying the lights of Midtown Manhattan and playing with the ends of her hair. Her profile was classic, high cheekbones and a narrow nose. Despite not wearing any makeup she had thick eyelashes, most likely courtesy of her Italian heritage. True to her earlier words, she had put her slippers back on and was still wearing them.

She was very comfortable naked, which I appreciated.

Skimming my hand over her cheek, I traced her jawline, and her bottom lip.

She did turn then and look at me, her expression thoughtful but relaxed.

For a split second, with her face caught in the city lights, I felt something I didn't want to feel. Something deep and powerful and fucking earth-shattering.

But then she stuck her tongue out at me.

The moment evaporated and I laughed, grateful for her silly gesture. She'd saved me from falling down a hole I couldn't climb out of and sure as hell didn't want to be in.

I bent down and kissed her.

Not a light, teasing kiss.

Not a tender kiss.

But a hard, demanding kiss to make me forget that I could

be vulnerable to the beauty of a woman. To remind myself that a relationship wasn't in our future and that I had no business roping Leah into dealing with me, the cold workaholic who would always put work first.

I ran my hands over her body, touching her warm, soft flesh everywhere, stroking her to sweet little gasps of pleasure.

Then I lifted her fuzzy fleece slippers onto my shoulder and I plunged inside her, hard and demanding.

I wanted to distract myself from thinking.

Drown in pleasure.

And convince myself that this was nothing. That I felt nothing. That we were nothing.

So I gripped her calves with a tight punishing hold and lied to myself.

CHAPTER 9

Something felt different about Grant.

We were lying in his bed and it was sexy and intimate, our bodies spent. Yet he seemed to have left behind the easy, teasing mood from dinner and was quiet. He'd gotten a notification on his phone and he'd actually looked at it, which seemed like poor post-sex etiquette.

Feeling left out of whatever the hell he was looking at, I'd picked up my own phone and started scrolling through social media.

"Hey, look, that video of me singing in Chanel is still up." I showed it to Grant.

He took my phone out of my hand. I wasn't expecting him to do that.

"Um, grabbie," I complained.

"Sorry, but I can't see it when you hold it. Your hand is moving." Grant held the phone up over his head and clicked the play button.

My voice filled his bedroom. I was used to having recordings of me singing, but something about this felt so surreal. The lights of Manhattan penetrated the darkness of Grant's bedroom and his sheets were cool, our naked bodies warm.

"You sound fantastic. And look beautiful." He scrolled my screen. "Ten thousand likes."

"Ten thousand?" That stunned me. "Are you kidding? That's a lot."

"There are lots of positive comments too. Which isn't surprising. Like I said, you sound fantastic."

"Weird. It doesn't seem like something that would go viral." It didn't seem like that interesting of a video.

"I wouldn't call this viral," Grant said.

Okay, then. "Way to burst my bubble."

"Sorry, that's not what I meant. It's just viral is usually like millions of views. I'm sure you could go viral."

I knew he didn't mean it that way, but it felt like a slap in the face. A dream-crushing reality statement.

"No, I can't." I reached up and took my phone back. "I'm not a six-year-old sounding like Judy Garland. I'm not someone with an interesting story. I'm just another okay-looking, okay-singing twentysomething trying to find a job in entertainment. From an industry perspective, there is nothing interesting about me whatsoever. I don't stand out."

It was rare that I allowed myself to indulge in negativity. Truthfully, I didn't even feel that way very often. I had been born an optimist. But even though I doubted he'd meant to hurt me, it had just seemed so obvious that I was fighting an uphill battle because he was right. Viral videos are viewed millions of times, and here I was about ten thousand and shocked even by that volume. The difference was insurmountable.

"You don't have to wear a meat dress to stand out. Talent stands out, Leah."

Maybe it was being in his apartment. Maybe it was all those boxes of designer clothes in the other room waiting to be packed into luggage that cost thousands of dollars. Maybe it was Grant's confidence. Not just in his career, his life. Confidence that I would take this "job." That I would agree to come over tonight. Maybe it was that now he seemed a little reserved. Maybe it was all of those things.

But I felt worried that maybe my talent wasn't all it was cracked up to be.

Which was precisely why I hadn't wanted to date a rich guy.

Not that I was. I was fake dating a rich guy.

I was also draped over his hard, masculine chest, with a sore body from sex.

I hit the pause button on the video. I didn't want to hear my voice anymore. "Sure, it does," I said. "In a fantasy world." I tossed my phone on the nightstand and tried to shake my unexpected mood. "I'm thirsty. I'm going to get a glass of water. Do you want one too? Also, we should get started packing. That's a lot of boxes out there."

Grant reached for my arm as I sat up. "Hey. You okay? I didn't mean to hurt your feelings. That sounded a lot like I'm a total dickhead, and I swear, I didn't mean it that way. I spoke without thinking."

He looked concerned.

Which actually made me feel worse. He felt sorry for me.

"It's totally fine. It wasn't you. It was the video that reminded me of things I don't necessarily like to think about. Now let's not worry about any of that and just enjoy our night together. I still have half of my sangria to drink." I gave him a smile. Mostly fake, but partially real. "I keep getting distracted by a certain sexy real estate developer."

"Do I know him?" Grant said, looking relieved that I was letting him off the hook for his unintentionally thoughtless comment. "I'll crush the competition."

"He's great in bed," I warned. "It's a lot to live up to."

Grant threw the bedding off and stood up. He strolled across his bedroom and into his bathroom. "I'm not worried. I'm taking a shower. Care to join me?"

I did and I didn't. I would love the distraction, and well, all that hard, muscular nakedness rubbing up against me. But at the same time, I needed a minute alone to regroup. "Not this time."

Pulling my sweatshirt on, I fished around in the bedding until I found my panties and put those on as well. I went into the living room and busied myself cleaning up our takeout food. I washed the wok and wiped down the countertop. Then I started methodically transferring clothing into the luggage. It was mindless and made me feel accomplished.

I used the tissue between layers of clothing, and found nooks and crannies for all the boxes of jewelry. When all the shopping bags were emptied, I started folding them down and wondered what the hell Grant was doing. I felt better. It had been a brief pity party that I had come home early from. What was I worried about? I could pay my bills, comfortably now thanks to Grant's job offer, and I had friends and endless opportunities in my dream town.

It was all good.

Luggage all zipped up and resting against the wall, I went in search of Grant, wondering if he had drowned in the shower or fallen asleep. He was in the second bedroom, which was set up as an office. He was sitting behind the desk, at his laptop. He wasn't wearing a shirt and I suspected he was totally naked.

"Hey," he said, glancing up at me. "Sorry. Something came up at work and I had to address it. Are you all packed?"

"Yep. Many expensive garments ready to roll out for a forty-eight-hour trip." I went around the desk and glanced at his computer.

It was an aerial view of a portion of the city. For some reason, it looked familiar to me. "Where is that?" I asked. What was it about that one block? "Show me the street view."

"It's nothing," he said. "Just a development project downtown." He closed his laptop with a definitive slap. "I shouldn't be working when I have such a fascinating houseguest."

"I can't argue with that."

Grant spun his chair around so he was facing me instead of the desk. He had a towel wrapped around his waist. I sat down on his lap, spreading my legs on either side of him. I tugged on his beard and shifted my hips so important parts of me were touching parts of him. "You should pack," I murmured.

"I should." His hands gripped my waist and he pulled me closer against him. "And we need to get you some pants or that's never going to happen. Because your body is very, very tempting."

I backed off, making sure to wiggle my ass over every inch of his lap as I did before standing up. "I don't want to be responsible for you not packing. Get to it."

Grant stood up, and as I was intending to exit the room, he took my hand. "Hey. I want to apologize again for my insensitive comment. I know you work really hard and I want you to know how much I respect your tenacity and your talent."

I turned and gave him a little nod. But I couldn't stop myself from wrapping my arms over my chest, wondering how much I should reveal to Grant. I decided to be honest, because it wasn't going to shock him. It was just the reality of being a struggling actress in New York. I never revealed my fear, and I was going to downplay it here, but he clearly felt bad. And I wanted him to understand, wanted him to know that I wasn't like him. Doors wouldn't magically open for me.

"I know you didn't mean anything. It's okay. Like I said, it's just sometimes I wonder where to go from here. My parents thought I was insane to want to move to the city. My mother thought I was going to be murdered and my father worried some asshole director would sexually harass me. They both thought I was going to starve and live in a rat-infested apartment. The only thing they were wrong about was I was not murdered," I said wryly. "But I've gotten to what I consider a reasonable place of self-sufficiency but that concern for survival is still there. It will always be there. I don't even care about being a huge star or being famous. I just want to be able to do what I love and pay my bills. Chorus girl in a long-running show would be a dream job for me. But what if that never even happens?" I shrugged.

"What if it does?" Grant asked simply. "And if it doesn't, you just said you're in a reasonable place, so what is wrong with that? I know that I've had a huge advantage in life, so I don't come from the same place as you do, but I do know that most people achieve success after a lot of hard work and grinding determination. You have that kind of moxie, Leah. I've seen it."

Did I have moxie? I thought I did. I wanted to believe I did, and God, there was something so sweet about the billionaire giving me a pep talk. With my friends, it was hard to be vulnerable or afraid because I felt responsible for dragging them down with me. If I said it was impossible to succeed in New York, that was spitting on their dreams too, and I couldn't do that. But if I spoke the truth to Grant, I wasn't going to affect his morale. He might actually be a safe person to confide in.

"Do you want to know my worst fear? And I don't mean roaches," I said. If I wanted Grant to know me, the real me, this was an important part of what motivated me. Or maybe, what held me back.

And for whatever reason, I did want Grant to know the real me. He kept asking which was the real me and which was the actress speaking. Well, this was the truth. What I'd already said and what I was going to dig just a little deeper into.

"Yes," Grant said. "If you're willing to share."

"My fear is total failure. That I won't even get small parts anymore. I'll just be going and going, trying to make this work, then one day I wake up and realize it will never happen. And then what? Because all of my friends moved in different directions and they've found success. I don't have any other talents or skills. There is no backup plan. None. I'm not great at anything other than pretending to be what I'm not. That's terrifying."

"If you've never tried anything else how do you know you're not good at anything? I think you're underselling yourself."

"No. Trust me. I am not good at numbers, or selling things, or crafting, or dealing with children. I can't make soap or jewelry, I don't have a degree that would allow me to tutor or teach, and I feel woozy at the sight of blood or needles so anything in the medical industry is out. What am I supposed to do?" All of that made my throat tighten and my eye twitch. I squeezed my arms tighter around me.

"Leah. Look at me." He put his hands on my upper arms and gently rubbed.

I tried to stop panicking and met Grant's penetrating gaze. "What?"

"If there's no other option, then your only option is success. Nikki Sixx from Mötley Crüe always said he had no other plan. There was no backup so he had to make music work. That's the way you have to approach it. There's no giving up, there's no searching for an out. You're all in. You're my little Nikki Sixx."

It made me feel warm inside, both because Grant was trying to encourage me and because I felt like he really listening to me. That he got me.

His little Nikki Sixx. *His.*

I could fall in love with Grant. I realized it suddenly, with one shocking wave of lightheadedness and hot cheeks. I *was* falling in love with Grant.

What hadn't upset me was just his saying the video wasn't technically viral, it was also that he had pulled back from me. It had felt a little dismissive and that had bothered me because my heart was getting drawn into this fake relationship with Grant.

Oh, shit. Where was my self-preservation?

How could I be so blind? I'd been heading for this moment since I'd chased him and gotten hit by a cab and he'd peeled me off the street.

I'd talked to him, flirted with him, every day. I'd confessed my deepest fear.

Not a fake relationship, Leah. Way to ensure your heart is thoroughly shattered. Good job.

I focused on his statement of total confidence. "Success is my only option, huh?" I said. "I'm not sure if that's encouraging or terrifying, but thank you. I appreciate you listening to me. You're a good man, Grant."

He shook me a little. "You've got this, Leah. I would bet Vegas odds on you."

I took a deep breath. I was so far in, it wasn't that I had a choice. I couldn't switch gears on my career now. I could however, save myself from falling head over ass for Grant.

Keep it light. "Well, I don't want you to lose your shirt so I guess I'll keep at it."

Grant kissed my forehead. "You're badass and don't forget it. You got hit by a cab and took it on the chin."

That made me smile, even when I didn't want to. "True."

"Can I tell you something?" he asked, shifting his hands into mine and pulling my arms down by my sides.

"What?"

"I lied when I said I don't have any fears."

That startled me and I didn't say anything, just waited. I had a feeling Grant was about to reveal a truth he didn't share with a lot of people, if anyone.

I wanted to hear what he was going to say. I needed to hear it. I was afraid to hear it.

Maybe it would be something horrible that would save me from the torment of falling in love with him.

Or maybe it would seal the deal and I would be screwed.

I couldn't believe I was going to get real with Leah.

But she had been honest and vulnerable and not only did it seem unfair to her to let her think that I was a man without any baggage, I felt like she wasn't like my family and co-workers. She wasn't going to judge me or scoff or perceive me displaying any emotion at all as a sign of weakness. I had learned a long time ago in my life that the smartest form of protection was icy indifference.

I didn't want to be either icy or indifferent with Leah.

"I've spent most of my life alone," I told her. "And sometimes I think I'm going to be like Ebenezer Scrooge, old and surrounded by wealth, but nothing else."

Holy fuck, I'd said it out loud and the earth hadn't opened up and swallowed me. She wasn't rolling her eyes or laughing or acting like I was ridiculous.

Instead she squeezed my hands and said, "You had a lonely childhood, didn't you?"

I nodded. "Yes. My parents were never around and I wasn't really allowed to mingle much with other kids, except at the park. Rose was my only constant, and then my mother fired her when I was twelve because she thought I was too old for a nanny. Which I was." The memory still made my nostrils flare and my stomach clench. "But Rose was my mother, for all practical and emotional purposes. And they cut me off from the only person who had ever loved me and wouldn't even let me interact with her."

"Oh, God, that's horrible." Leah's thumbs gently rubbed over the backs of my hands. "I can't even imagine." She did look horrified. "Why weren't you allowed to see her?"

"My mother said my affection for Rose was unnatural." I shook my head. "Apparently, it's fine to love your nanny at five years old but at twelve my mother deemed it weird. So Rose disappeared and I got sent to boarding school."

And that was the day I stopped caring about trying to gather my parents' love and started doing what I wanted.

"That's just cruel, Grant. I'm so sorry." She kissed me softly.

"But you can choose to live your life now however you want. You don't have to be Ebenezer. You're not a Scrooge now, I can tell you that. You've been nothing but considerate of my ankle injury and generous with tips and gifts. I think you're a good guy. You can love your job and work long hours and still be a man with a personal life."

Maybe she had a point. Maybe I wasn't as cold-hearted as I thought I was sometimes.

My moral compass was way more on target than my mother's, that was for sure. I avoided relationships so I didn't hurt anyone. Maybe who I was hurting was mostly myself.

"That's true in theory, but I'm not good at the juggling act and I don't want to hurt someone. Especially not someone I care about." Like her. Like Leah.

Leah tilted her head and those expressive eyes studied me. "Grant. Don't make an adult woman's choice for her. If she wants to love you, let her. She's a big girl and knows that any relationship carries the risk of being hurt."

Was she talking about herself? I had no fucking clue.

All I knew was that I *wanted* her to be talking about herself.

I wasn't going to go there though. Not yet. Maybe after this weekend we could move into something… else. Something more. Something that wasn't fake.

"As a side note, I defied my parents and found Rose living in Florida with her adult son. I booked myself a first-class ticket out of LaGuardia with my father's credit card and flew down there for Christmas break. I did that every year through middle school and high school and they never said shit about it." The memory did make me smile. "Rose made me chocolate chip pancakes every Christmas morning."

Leah's face softened as she realized now why I'd started coming to the diner. "Oh. That sounds like a wonderful way to spend Christmas."

I'd sliced open my chest and shown Leah my heart. Yes, she was gazing at me like she wanted to scoop up the little boy that I'd been and hug me. But there was also admiration in her expression. And neither of those responses made me uncomfortable. I didn't want to toss off an asshole comment and shut down the conversation.

I trusted her.

It was a fantastic feeling.

Which meant I needed to tell her I was intending to tear down the theater she loved if I wanted any chance of this being something.

But later.

After we got back from the Hamptons.

"It was." I kissed her knuckles and stepped back. "Now how about that drink?"

She pursed her lips together, like she was going to say something else.

I waited, tense.

But she just smiled. "I'm not packing your stuff. Don't think I am."

"I wouldn't dream of it. I am perfectly capable of packing for myself. Loner, remember?" I gestured around my apartment. "I take care of myself."

Leah's eyebrows shot up. "You clean your own apartment?"

Well. "Okay, so not that. I have a cleaning service. But, I make my own bed. Does that count for anything?"

"I'm impressed." Leah moved to the doorway. She turned, hair spilling down her back, her lean legs still bare beneath her sweatshirt. "I like talking to you. Just in case you were wondering."

My gut clenched. "I like talking to you too."

The rest of the night we stuck to banter, with Leah extoling the virtues of why she loved the movie Overboard as she stood in my closet and watched me pack. "How can anyone not love Goldie Hawn?"

"I do appreciate Goldie Hawn." There was no way in fucking hell I was going to admit I'd gone home after work that day she'd explained her "Hi, Grant!" routine and had watched the movie. Nope. Never going to happen.

"How is it her character is such a bitch in the beginning but you still just find her hilarious?" Leah was sitting on the closet floor leaning against the doorframe. Her knees were up and tucked under her sweatshirt. Occasionally she would reach out and touch the hem of one of my pairs of pants that were hanging to the left of her.

"I don't know. Good acting, I guess." I opened the drawer that housed my socks and pulled out what was necessary. It felt intimate as hell to have her watching me pack. Plenty of women had seen me unpack in a hotel room, but no one had been in my closet while I packed.

At least Leah wouldn't be lying about half the things she might say to my parents. She probably knew more about me than ninety-five percent of people in my life.

That thought had me slamming the drawer shut.

Now that was a fucked-up statement.

At least I could reassure myself she knew nothing about my work. It seemed important that I remain elusive on some level otherwise I'd really be in trouble.

Again, a fucked-up statement.

"Do you think it's possible to forgive someone for lying about something as huge as who you are? Like she forgives Kurt Russell even though he gave her a completely false identity in order to have her clean his house. Could you forgive someone for that?"

That was a hell of a lie. "My gut reaction is hell no. How about you?"

"I don't know. It depends on the context."

Maybe she would forgive me then for withholding the information that I was trying to buy the theater. To tear it down. That wasn't horrible in the grand scheme of things. More like an omission, not an actual lie.

Not that it mattered.

We had a business deal. Nothing more.

Even if I didn't believe that anymore.

"Then you're a better person than me if you can forgive a man telling you you're a totally different person, who has children, when in fact, you don't."

"You did watch the movie! I knew it." She grinned at me.

Shit. "You don't know that."

"Yes, I do. I am the wisest woman in the world, according to you."

That made me laugh. "I said that under the influence of you naked. You can't hold me to that."

"Bullshit. You adore me, just admit it."

I wasn't going to admit that any more than I was that I'd watched Overboard. Our truth time was over for the night.

"You're someone I don't object to spending time with."

Leah let out a peal of laughter. "You know how to flatter a girl."

"That's why you love being my fake girlfriend."

"It doesn't suck."

I closed my suitcase and zipped it. I eased past Leah, making sure my legs brushed against her and she was eye level with my cock. "Sorry. Excuse me."

"You're lucky you're wearing pants."

"Why, were you going to make my day?" I would love to see her get on her knees and…

"If squeezing your balls would make your day, then yes."

Not what I was hoping. Even though I knew she was just giving me shit, it still made me wince a little. "Oh, hey, hey now. Let's leave the boys out of this."

Leah laughed. "Calm down. Give me a hand. I need one more teeny tiny glass of wine, then I'm ready for bed. What time are we leaving tomorrow?"

I helped her off the floor. "Noon-ish. So we can sleep in. Or you know, do other things before we leave."

"What things?" She gave me a cheeky look. "Make breakfast?"

"We can do that. Or we can go to the restaurant across the street. Or we can skip breakfast and spend the entire morning in bed."

"I'm not a morning person."

Now she was just being contrary. She worked in the morning. She was always cheerful and on at the diner.

"What you are is sassy." I went to pull her against me, but she shrieked and ran away from me, laughing.

"Where are you going?"

Leah peeled her sweatshirt off. The damn thing was like a theater curtain. Huge and covering the stage. When it rose, it was showtime. I took two hard steps toward her, but she climbed onto my bed and stretched in a glorious display of skin and curves.

"I changed my mind," she said with a sweet smile. "I think it's time for bed. I'm so tired."

I had on basketball shorts and nothing else and I ditched those in two seconds. "If you're tired, then yes, we should definitely go to bed."

"Can we cuddle?"

"Oh, fuck yeah, we cuddle. I'll cuddle you in a way you've never been cuddled before."

The corner of her mouth turned up in a sly, seductive smile. "Why, Grant, you sweet talker you."

I realized, as I climbed on the bed, I had no idea what Leah was actually thinking.

All I knew was that I was thinking she looked damn good in my bed and I never wanted her to leave.

CHAPTER 10

I didn't sleep at all. Or very little, anyway. I stared at my ceiling and I stared at Leah and I stared out the damn window wondering what the hell was going on with my feelings and wondering what the hell I was supposed to do about it.

Leah was sleeping peacefully, her dark hair spilling over the white of the pillowcase. I'd never had a woman spend the night here. If I stayed with a hookup, it was always at her place. I didn't like women in my private space, my sanctuary. Yet Leah had invaded my apartment with her teasing and her laughter and her soft moans. I didn't mind. I liked it. She made the space feel alive in a way it hadn't before.

I was lying there debating how to climb out of bed without waking her up when my phone buzzed. The sneakers I'd ordered for Leah the night before were downstairs at the front desk. We could grab them on our way out.

My phone woke Leah up. She sighed and rolled over toward me, resting her hand on my chest. Her eyes were still closed. "What time is it?" she murmured.

"It's early. You can keep sleeping." I ran my hand over her back, wondering what it would feel like to wake up next to Leah on a regular basis.

Something monumental had happened. There was no denying it and my intentions had shifted.

I was weighing the pros and cons of a relationship in my mind. I was negotiating with myself like it was a damn business deal. Return on investment. Risk factors. Initial start-up costs. I wanted a numerical calculation to tell me if it would be a solid venture or not but surprise. Relationships don't fucking work like that. There was no formula that would give me the potential success rate of dating Leah.

I rubbed my hand over my beard and decided I was an asshole.

"Are you awkward about morning breath or am I allowed to kiss you?" Leah asked.

She had pried her eyes open and was giving me a sleepy smile. What man on the planet would turn down a kiss from a face that freaking adorable? I didn't answer, just cupped her cheek and pressed my lips to hers.

"Mm. That's nice," she said. "Beach or mountains?"

"Beach." I didn't even need to ask what she meant. She was continuing twenty questions. "You?"

"Beach. Would you rather go to outer space or down into the depths of the ocean?"

"Good one. Huh. The ocean."

"Outer space."

"What were you doing a year ago today?"

"Specifically, today? As in this date or this particular Friday in October?"

"Either one."

"I don't remember exactly. But working on a project in SoHo. Redevelopment of retail space to condos. What were you doing?"

She laughed. "Not this. I was working and I had an audition for a Broadway show right around this time. I didn't get the part."

"What will you be doing next year at this time?" I asked.

Leah wrinkled her nose. "I don't even want to think about it."

Because we'd both probably be doing the same thing. Exactly what we'd been doing last year and should be doing this year if it wasn't for my parents' party.

Unless I opened my mouth and made something different happen.

But before I could think of what, if anything, I wanted to say, Leah climbed out of bed. "I need coffee."

I wasn't ready to change her mind.

And I didn't think she was ready to hear it.

For now, we were still faking it.

"This is Sagaponack," Grant said as we drove through a quaint little town of restaurants and shops.

There was lots of clapboard and cedar shingles. It didn't look outrageously wealthy, just very New England and for sure upscale, but not the flash of the West Coast.

"It's very cute. Did you spend a lot of time here?" I was glad he'd chosen to drive us personally instead of having his driver, though the interior of his sports car was like nothing I'd ever seen. There was no propping my feet on this dash in this luxury machine. It had been a calm drive, with easy conversation between us. It was always easy to talk to Grant.

"In the summers, yes."

As Grant drove through the town and out onto a road, the water appeared, along with massive houses sprawling behind manicured lawns and seafront grasses. "Wow. Okay, these are mansions," I said.

Grant glanced over at me. "These are bungalows in Sagaponack terms."

I was bouncing on my seat, excited. "This is like being on a movie set. It's so perfect it doesn't even look real."

"The water is gorgeous, isn't it?"

I nodded. "Is your parents' house by the water? Can we take a walk later?" I felt like a kid on vacation. I was out of the city. I hit the button so the window went down halfway. "I can smell the water, this is amazing. Fresh air. It's real." If anyone tries to tell you New York doesn't frequently smell like garbage and old fish, they're lying. Or they don't work on the block I do.

"The house is on the water. Trust me, my mother will tell you the house is shit. That she wants to tear it down and rebuild but they can't get the proper permits, and she only bought the house from her parents for the view. The truth is there is nothing wrong with the house, it's just not what she wants, but she actually prefers complaining to remodeling."

"Good information to have. So I should talk about how dated it is?" I gave him a grin.

"Oh my God, please don't." Then Grant tilted his head a little. "Actually, that might be funny. No, never mind. I don't want you to be intimidated by my mother but I don't want you to be outright rude either. That's her style."

"Got it. Don't be intimidated. Don't be rude. Got it. I've auditioned in front of some of the biggest egos in New York. I honestly think I can handle it." I did. If Grant and I were an actual couple I might be more nervous. Since we weren't, I just had the usual pre-show jitters that were more excitement than anxiety.

"Did I mention that my family calls me Eddie?"

"*Eddie?*" That did not fit him at all.

He nodded. "Too many Grants. Edward is my middle name."

"I'm not calling you Eddie."

"I don't expect you to. It was just a heads-up. Here it is," Grant said, pulling into a lane that led to an enormous Cape Cod. "Prepare to earn your paycheck."

Oh. Right. The money. For being a fake girlfriend.

Because this wasn't real. We weren't even actually friends. We weren't dating, getting to know each other. I'd been reminding myself of that the entire time, but why was it jarring when Grant said it?

I knew why and I'd been wrestling with it for twenty-four

hours like it was an alligator and I was knee-deep in the bayou.

It was jarring because I didn't want it to be fake anymore. I wanted it to be real. Not kind of, but from the depths of my soul. Which was stupid, because nothing was different than before. Yes, I'd gotten to know Grant a little better and I enjoyed his company, but he was still a rich workaholic who was used to buying whatever he wanted and was resistant to a relationship. I was an optimistic financially strapped actress (though not so much anymore thanks to him, hence half the issue) who also didn't want a relationship because I needed to focus on my career now.

And yet... my insides felt like the creamy center of a truffle. Gooey.

But not only was it fake, it was a contractual agreement. That I had signed, insisting that we not have sex the entire weekend.

I swallowed the sudden lump in my throat. "Let's do this thing!" I said in an attempt to be casual and instead just sounding flippant and slightly manic. "Is there a butler? Please tell me there's a butler." Or was that just a British thing?

"There's no butler. That's only at the house in Turks & Caicos."

"Too bad the party isn't there." Now that would be a killer weekend. Especially if it was just me and Grant and a personal butler. Which, of course, would not serve the purpose of him bringing a fake girlfriend to trot in front of his parents.

"We usually have Christmas there." Grant opened his door and got out. He came around and opened my door, holding out a hand for me.

I rubbed my lips together and smoothed down my hair.

"Showtime."

"Don't let anything throw you for a curve," he said. "Just remember my entire family is insane."

That made me laugh. "Got it." I lifted up the clutch I'd found in the many boxes of accessories. I couldn't exactly show up with a backpack on. Not in character.

I sort of expected the door to open and to walk in and find an assembly line of relatives or maybe staff, Downton Abbey style. No one opened the door. No one was inside the foyer when Grant opened it. Not one relative. Not a maid. Not even a dog.

It was monstrously disappointing.

It had the feel and echo of a museum and I was thrust back into grade school when I was excited as hell to take a field trip and get out of the classroom only to learn it was to the historical society and I was expected to be quiet and not touch things. If there are two rules I am destined to break, they are "Be quiet" and "Don't touch." I'd ended up in serious trouble on that field trip after Nev Patel dared me to lick the fruit wallpaper and I did.

The same thing was bound to happen here. I was going to break the rules at some point and lick something. Or at least say something I shouldn't.

"Don't let my mother steamroll you," Grant said in a low voice as he ushered me in, our footsteps ringing on the marble floor.

His demeanor had changed the second he'd crossed the threshold. He was agitated instead of relaxed. Frowning instead of that easy smile I had gotten used to seeing.

"Grant." I touched his arm. "Relax. It's going to be okay. We might even have fun."

He eyed me. "Oh, you are an optimist, Leah. Let's see how you feel on Sunday."

"I'm feeling good about everything." I put my arm through his. "What happens now? Do we ring a bell or yell 'shout at the devil' or something?"

"No bell ringing necessary," a man's voice said from above us.

I looked up and saw a man in his sixties coming down the prominent staircase. It was clearly Grant's father. I could see the resemblance. In front of him was a very thin and very tall woman. She moved easily down the stairs, like she was used to being the center of attention.

"You must be the infamous Leah," she said as she hit the marble floor at the bottom of the stairs. "I'm Grant's mother."

If I had been expecting a hug, there wasn't one in sight. I tried to imagine how that lack of affection would feel if I really was Grant's girlfriend. Not good. She didn't put her hand out either, or offer her first name. Apparently, I was supposed to refer to her as "Grant's mother."

"It's a pleasure to meet you," I said.

Her response? "Uh-huh." She presented her cheek to Grant for a kiss and he obliged.

"Mother." He turned to me. "You can call my mother Tiffany, by the way. I think she forgot to mention that."

His father did offer his hand to me. "Welcome, Leah. We're happy to meet you. This guy has been hiding you for far too long."

"Thank you. I'm happy to be here and congratulations, by the way. Thirty-five years of marriage is amazing."

For whatever reason his mother made a sniffing sound. I had no idea what was so offensive about what I'd said. I was just going to smile my way through this.

"Thank you. It's been quite a ride, right, Tiff? You can call me Grant," his father said.

Yeah, that felt weird. It was not going to happen. Considering how often I had said that name while moaning in pleasure I could not look Grant's father in the face and call him the same.

I just shook his hand and smiled. "Thank you for inviting me."

"Remind me again what you do for a living?" Tiffany asked.

She was wearing an outfit that was clearly designer, though I couldn't tell you which one. It just looked expensive. *She* looked expensive, reminding me of a purebred Afghan hound with her long silken hair and elegant posture. I was more like a mutt mix that bounded into a room.

Also, did she really forget in a matter of a week that I was a server? Doubtful. She just wanted me to say it out loud. I knew Grant had told his parents a little bit about me.

"I'm a server," I said. And no apology necessary. It's a demanding job that requires a great deal of skill. Not to mention reading people. I was reading Tiffany and she was one rich bitch. Grant had all but said it and I could practically smell privilege wafting off of her like Chanel number five.

"A server? What's that?" Grant's father asked.

I thought maybe he was being facetious but I wasn't sure. Grant didn't seem to think so. "Waitress, Dad. But you know, in modern terminology."

"Oh. Sure." He didn't seem to know what to say to that.

Grant's mother did.

"A waitress? How does a waitress afford Prada?" Tiffany eyed me up and down with disdain.

This was going to go well.

Grant had said don't let her steamroll me.

"Grant is very generous," I said, trying to channel a Southern woman at a church brunch. I wanted to "bless your heart" his mother so much. But it was just internal inspiration. I wasn't supposed to be Southern.

"I see. So you're a gold digger."

Straight to the point. I vowed not to eyeroll.

"Mom!" Grant shot his mother a glare. "Stop it."

I gave Tiffany Caldwell an easy smile. "Of course I'm a gold digger," I said. "Because it can't possibly be that I'm attracted to Grant because he's charming, intelligent, or good looking. That he's kind and funny and is absolutely fantastic in bed. Which he is. *Fantastic.* I mean, my God, I've never had a lover like him. The money is nice too, but his enormous—"

His mother held her hand up. "You've made your point."

Grant's father let out a crack of laughter. "I think you've met your match, Tiff. You don't scare Leah. Now let's get out of the hallway and have a drink. Eddie, where's your luggage?"

Hearing Grant referred to as Eddie was as jarring as hearing his father called Grant. The man standing next to me was not an Eddie. Edward, sure. Eddie, no.

"It's in the car. I'll get it later."

"You're staying in the north bedroom," Tiffany said.

The frown on Grant's face made it clear he hadn't been expecting to be assigned the north bedroom.

The undercurrent in the room was tension. "A drink sounds fabulous," I said.

But as we followed his parents into an expansive great room, Grant shook his head at me. "What?" I murmured.

"My dad over pours. Sip very slowly."

It was clear Grant Caldwell the second liked his cocktails. The bar was elaborate and fully stocked. I wanted to check out the view and the house but I decided to keep an eye on my drink being poured. It was a good thing I did. My lemon drop was a quarter of a bottle of vodka with one begrudging little splash of simple syrup and a lemon wedge.

We sat down on plush sofas that faced the view of the water. I took a tentative sip of my drink and felt my insides burn with pure alcohol.

"Where's Gigi and Grandpa?" Grant asked his mother.

"They're napping before dinner."

"Oh, okay. What are the dinner plans?"

"I thought we'd go to town since tomorrow is the party. I refuse to lift a finger today."

Somehow, I doubted Tiffany Caldwell lifted a finger any day unless it was to one-click a purchase on her phone.

"Your house is lovely. What an amazing view."

Tiffany waved her hand. "Oh, God, this house is horrible. I've been telling my husband for years we need to renovate. But all these rules and permits and regulations. I can't deal with it."

Just like Grant had said.

"At least the location is fantastic," I said cheerfully, determined to play "girlfriend trying to impress her boyfriend's mother."

No joke, his mother muttered, "Whatever. Of course, *you* would think so."

Like she was twelve.

That was so not necessary. Not to mention bitchy and childish.

It made me more determined than ever to kill Tiffany with kindness.

Especially given that Grant looked pissed. He actually reached over and took my hand into his and gave it a squeeze. His nostrils were flaring and he looked like he was fighting the urge to say something. I squeezed back to reassure him.

Why did I care if his mom was being ridiculous? I really didn't.

Grant's father had already drained about half of his cocktail, which was astonishing. I swear, I hadn't even seen him lift the glass more than once, so did he take all of that down with one sip? The very thought made my insides want to burst into flames. But the man probably needed to drink to cope with Tiffany. He was way more chill than his wife.

I decided to make him an ally.

"So how did you and Tiffany meet?" I asked him with a big smile.

Grant shifted on the sofa next to me and cleared his throat.

His father chuckled. His mother gave me a death stare.

"At a party here at this house, actually. Tiffany's parents owned it then and I had some friends who knew Tiff. We showed up just in time to see Tiff jump into the pool off the roof. Naked. I fell for her right then and there."

"Wow. How agile," I said. "I'm impressed. I would be terrified to jump off the roof." I wasn't lying about that. You couldn't pay me to jump into a pool from a rooftop. Naked would be fine. Though maybe not in front of a whole party crowd. But I would certainly swim naked with a boyfriend.

"Grant, why do you have to tell that ridiculous story? My God, it was the eighties. Everyone was jumping off roofs naked. If there wasn't cocaine and promiscuity it wasn't even a real party."

I would lay down money that is not what my parents had been doing in the eighties. More like a keg party with flipped collars at the very most.

"I miss the eighties," his father said in a joking voice.

I couldn't help it. I laughed.

CHAPTER 11

So far, the weekend was going exactly as expected. My father was half in the bag already and my mother was pouting for no apparent reason whatsoever.

I was resigned to suffer through until we could escape to the north bedroom, which was some sort of statement on my mother's part. It was the shittiest guest room in the house, facing the garage. My mom never put anyone in that room unless the house was totally full and she was making a statement about the person's status. I wasn't sure if the gesture was meant to be a slight against me or against Leah.

I'd heard the naked pool party story a thousand times so that didn't bother me. At the anniversary party, it was bound to be retold tomorrow. My father absolutely loved the story because it made him look like a baller who landed the hot and wild chick. My mother pretended to hate the story, but I secretly thought she was just angry there was no video footage of it. She was not a woman who regretted her youth—she missed it.

When I was thirteen and they told that story, it had been different. I'd been painfully embarrassed. Thank God the phrase MILF wasn't in popular existence yet. All of my friends would have loved to give me shit about that. I had often thought in hindsight one of the reasons I'd felt comfortable with Trevor right away was that he wasn't sexually interested in my mom like ninety percent of my other friends.

"I'm hoping no one is jumping off the roof at your party tomorrow," I said, and I was only half kidding. "You're liable if someone gets hurts."

"You're such a buzz kill," Mom said.

I'd take that. "I am. Completely. Ask Leah."

"How did you two kids meet?" my father asked Leah. "Online?"

"No. I walked into a diner and there she was, wearing a uniform. This angel singing Ava Maria in a poodle skirt while people shoveled eggs and waffles into their mouths." I'd always be fond of that poodle skirt.

"A poodle skirt? Good Lord, how can you stand a job that forces you to wear kitsch?"

"The tips are good," Leah said. "Especially when I sing."

"So she was your server?" Dad asked.

Note he had the language down now. I knew he'd been just being a smartass earlier.

"Yes. I sat at the bar."

"He was very serious. I didn't know what to make of him."

Leah leaned against me, in full-on girlfriend role.

"After eating there twice, I decided to ask her out. So that's what happened."

"What he actually said was 'Why don't you come to my place for dinner and stay forever?'"

My story was boring, I could admit that, but really? She had to make me sound like a complete tool? I looked down at her and shot her a look, but I was more amused than annoyed.

"Eddie. Jesus." Dad sounded amused. "Going right for it. Like your old man."

"He's smooth like Skippy," Leah said.

I didn't mean to. Hell, I didn't want to. But I burst out laughing because that was ridiculous. There was no telling what in the hell was going to come out of Leah's mouth.

Simultaneously both of my parents shot each other a look, like they couldn't believe I was laughing out loud. Which was fair enough. I did laugh. Just generally not in their company. Even then, I wasn't a jovial guy. No one would claim that.

"And I *really* like peanut butter," Leah said. "I couldn't resist him."

"So you're living together?" Dad asked.

He looked pleased by that. Alarm bells started to go off inside me. What if Leah said we were living together? Then again, what difference did it make? They never came to my apartment. In fact, in the two years I'd been living there, they had never seen it.

It didn't matter anyway. Leah was shaking her head.

"Oh, no, I didn't mean that. I need to know how serious he

is about our relationship. I know his track record. But I liked his confidence and his general cheesiness."

I looked at her. "That was a backhanded compliment."

Leah smiled up at me sweetly and scratched my beard. She just reached up and ran her fingers through it like we were alone. "Shh. It was not."

Speaking of confidence. Hers had no bounds.

It's not that I had expected Leah to be shy or demure. But I had thought she would just be cheerful, pleasant, compliant. I hadn't anticipated she would have this whole narrative laid out to present to my parents. In which she both managed to do the job I had hired her for and teased me mercilessly at the same time.

As I stared into her brown eyes, on the sofa at my parents' house in the Hamptons, and let her stroke my beard with total familiarity, I knew I was in trouble.

I was falling for Leah. For real.

And I didn't hate it.

I took her hand and kissed her fingers. One by one. While her eyes darkened.

Falling? That was a fucking lie. *Fallen.*

I had fallen for Leah.

"You certainly don't want to rush anything," my mother said, completely ruining the moment of intimacy.

Her voice was a harsh, grating, and negative reality in a moment that felt huge. The moment I was staring into Leah's eyes and thinking this could really be something.

And there was my mother, the nails on the chalkboard

destroying the vibe.

"You really don't know anything about this woman," she continued.

As if Leah wasn't sitting right there.

As if I were an idiot who couldn't make my own decisions about who to spend my time with.

I thought about Leah's response to me telling her about Rose. How sweet and understanding she had been and how easy it had been to talk to her.

Thirty years of irritation with my mother collided with the unexpected intensity of my feelings for Leah and I knew I couldn't spend the entire weekend listening to her pick at Leah for zero reason whatsoever. I needed to shut that shit down now.

"I know everything I need to know about Leah," I said in complete honesty. Then I turned to my mother and figuratively dropped the mic. "That's why I asked Leah to marry me."

Leah made a strangled sound, but I just squeezed her hand tighter in warning. My father choked on his gin. My mother frowned, giving me the evil eye.

"Excuse me?" she said. "You're engaged to this woman? Have you lost your mind?"

I stared her down. "Yes. I'm engaged to *this woman*. Whose name is Leah. She's a singer and a server and she's going to be my wife."

The word wife should have had me choking on my own spit. It didn't. It rang out loud and clear and determined. I felt the force of it down to the tips of my Italian leather shoes. For the first time ever, I could envision myself taking vows to love someone forever. To love Leah. It didn't feel awful or foreign or fucking terrifying. It felt like a goal.

Make it real. Make Leah mine.

My mother was holding her chest like she was having a heart attack and I knew I had about ten seconds before all hell broke loose.

I stood up, pulling Leah with me, who looked equally as stunned as my mother. "Let's go get our luggage, sweetheart."

I had just pulled one of my mother's moves. Walk into a room with a hand grenade. Pull the pin. Walk out, leaving destruction in your wake.

It felt good, I wasn't going to lie.

Until we got outside and Leah hissed, "Are you insane? We've been here ten minutes and you flipped the script!"

My high from both besting my mother and realizing the true depth of my feelings for Leah deflated just a little. Leah was clearly angry. I popped open the trunk. "It's called improv. I'm sure you've done it before. I had to shut my mother down or she was going to be intolerable all weekend to you. I thought she would at least attempt to behave but she was being pretentious and nasty so I threw her off. She won't say anything the rest of the visit."

"Give me a warning before you change anything. That's all I asked. The one thing!" She put her hands on her cheeks. "Oh my God, my face is on fire. I'm so embarrassed."

I smiled at her. "Embarrassed to be engaged to me?"

"We're not engaged! We're nothing. This isn't funny. I'm really mad at you!"

Her words were a kick in the dick. Nothing. We were nothing. She was right and I hated it. "No, you're not mad at me. How can you be? What difference does it make? It's a business deal and I just renegotiated the terms. I'll increase your rate if you want."

I added that because her words had seriously bothered me. It was a knee-jerk childish reaction but the words were already out before I could stop them.

Her mouth dropped. Then her eyes narrowed. "Oh, really? If you can change the rules, then so can I. Watch out, Grant Caldwell the third. Your mother is right—you don't know a thing about this woman."

I felt the first ounce of concern. "What does that mean?"

Leah went up on tiptoes and ran her lips along my earlobe before whispering, "Never tell an angry woman she isn't angry." Then she bit my ear. Hard.

Leah took the smallest bag out of the trunk and spun on her heel and strolled back into the house.

Oh, yeah. I was so in love with her.

What the frickety-frack was Grant thinking? I carried the suitcase into the house, cheeks on fire, mind racing. Engaged. To be his wife. Oh my God. The man had lost his mind.

Of course, the reason I was so upset was because it was hard enough to play the role of his girlfriend and know it was fake. But fake fiancée? It was like pretending to be a princess when in reality you're Cinderella. Cleaning up after other people while having a nonexistent love life. That was me. Nonexistent love life and a world where eight grand bought you a used car, not a pair of pants.

Had a part of me for one nanosecond wished that it were true? Oh, yeah. Totally. Which is why it sucked so hard. My stupid heart had lifted like a helium balloon for a beat, then had fallen down into my gut. It wasn't real and I had never wanted to get married anyway, so why did any of it matter?

Grant was right about that. Why did it matter?

Except that it did and I was both angry with him for catching me off guard and angry with myself for feeling things I had no business feeling.

I strode into the living room. "Sorry to be a bother." Not really. "Which room would you like us to stay in?" I needed a minute alone to stop being overly invested in the situation. To pull back.

"The north bedroom," Tiffany said.

That helped me exactly not at all. I was tempted to roll my eyes. You'd think she would at least pride herself on being a decent hostess but she was actually in a full recline on the sofa now and showed no sign of standing up anytime soon. Grant's father was mixing himself another drink.

"Where is my son?" Tiffany asked. "I need a word with him."

"I'm right here," Grant said. "I'm going to take Leah up to our room."

"Take her up then come back. Alone." She dramatically put her hand across her forehead. "I need you to promise me that thing you said was a joke."

"It's not," he said flatly.

He hadn't lied. His mother really was horrible. She spoke like I wasn't in the room.

"I want to go swimming," I said, before Tiffany could speak. "Grant, take me to the pool so we can practice our dance for our wedding reception. There's a certain lift you promised me." I gave him a brilliant smile.

I figured that statement would punish him and his mother both.

I didn't have a swimsuit but his mother was irritating enough that I just might be tempted to go skinny-dipping.

It didn't take Grant long to react. There was a brief pause where he seemed to be assessing if I were serious or not, then he nodded. "Of course, sweetheart. We want our wedding to be perfect."

Tiffany hauled herself to a sitting position. "No one in this family is doing one of those tacky coordinated dances. I forbid it."

"Tiff, you did cocaine with Mötley Crüe at our wedding. I think a coordinated dance is perfectly acceptable compared to that."

Tiffany glared at Grant's father. "This whole weekend is ruined. My child hates me and my husband is an ass." She pointed a nail at Grant. "I'm disowning you." She turned to her husband. "And I want a divorce."

"No can do," Grant the second said cheerfully. "I dropped three hundred grand on this party, Tiff. We can't cancel it now."

"We'll call it a divorce party instead. We can announce we're disowning Grant."

"You can't disown me," Grant said. "My trust is from Gigi and Grandpa."

"What about me?" An older man entered the room from what appeared to be the library.

"Mom wants to cut me off," Grant said. "Because I'm getting married."

"To a gold digger!" his mother said. "She admitted it right to my face!"

I just stood there, convinced we were on a reality TV show. Who acted like this?

Apparently, billionaires.

"Tiff wants to divorce me too," Grant the second said.

"Oh, Christ, that's the most idle threat I've ever heard in my life. She's been saying that since the day after you got married. I wish she'd just do it already so we can stop talking about it." The man came over to me and stuck out his hand. "I'm Grant the first. You must be Eddie's new girlfriend."

I nodded. "I'm Leah. It's a pleasure to meet you."

He waved his hand behind him. "They're fucking crazy. Just so you know. My business acumen and work ethic skipped a generation. You've got a good man in Eddie."

I tried to imagine my grandfather dropping an f-bomb and couldn't fathom it.

"I totally agree. Eddie is a dream."

"You're getting married, huh? Congratulations. Welcome to the shit show."

That seemed legit. "Thank you."

"When's the big day?"

"Never," Tiffany said.

"We haven't really settled on a date," I said. "But it's going to be huge. Invite everyone we know. Spare no expense."

"I would love a spring wedding," Grant said.

I almost laughed. I wonder if he ever imagined words like that would ever come out of his mouth. He almost sounded believable. Almost. I was still mad at him, but this was kind of funny, I couldn't lie.

"Get her locked and loaded, eh, kid?" His grandfather tapped him on the shoulder. "Solid plan."

"It's a bullshit plan!" Tiffany yelled from the sofa.

Grant's grandfather raised an eyebrow and shook his head. "Fucking nuts. Can we get some food around here? I know Tiffany doesn't eat and Junior just drinks booze, but the rest of us would like a damn meal."

"The caterer has some trays in the refrigerator for today. Do you have any idea how exhausting it is to plan a party like this?" Tiffany said, sounding like she'd run a half marathon in ninety-degree heat.

"Especially when you haven't eaten in three years," Grant the first said. He shook his head at me. "Menopause hit that one hard. She's living on air to stay at that weight."

A slight woman in her seventies wandered in smoking a cigarette. "Who's in menopause?" she asked.

"Tiffany."

"Oh." She waved her hand in dismissal and took a drag. She was dressed like she was taking a stroll outside in January. Many layers of expensive wool and an elaborate headdress. "Who are you?" she asked me. "Are you one of Bert's kids? I seem to remember he married some Italian slut at some point. You look like her."

And wow. Just wow. "I'm not one of Bert's kids," I said. "I'm Grant's fiancée."

Her eyes narrowed. "Are you an Italian slut?"

"She's a waitress," Tiffany said.

"I don't think we should refer to other women as sluts," I said, unable to stop myself. If there is one thing I absolutely couldn't stand, it was women dragging down other women.

Gigi nodded. "Slut."

"Gigi!" Grant's voice roared loud and angry. "Don't you dare speak to her like that. This is my fiancée."

He sounded furious.

"Relax," Gigi said. "I didn't mean anything by it."

Really? And how was that exactly?

"We're going swimming," I said. "We'll see you all later at dinner." Or maybe we would skip dinner. I took Grant's hand and tugged him, moving backward.

When we got to the stairs, I just ran up them, no clue as to my destination. Grant grabbed a suitcase and followed suit. At the top of the stairs he turned left and opened the first door. He shoved it open so hard it bounced off the wall and hit him on the arm. He shoved it again and rolled the suitcase into the room.

"Fucking unbelievable," he said. "Can I disown all of *them*? They're insane."

I followed him into the room. "They're not great," I agreed. "I'm sorry." It was hard to stay mad at him when I pictured him as a small child being raised in a pack of jackals. It was a miracle he was even remotely normal.

He slammed the door shut and locked in. "No. I'm sorry for putting you in their line of fire." He reached out and brushed my hair off of my face. "I didn't think they would be amazing, but I didn't think they would be so insulting. This isn't fair to you. We can leave in the morning before the party. Hell, we can leave now if you want."

"I can handle it," I told him sincerely. "Eight years in the city has made me tougher than I look. We can do whatever you want. This is your position in the company at stake."

"But you're mad at me," he said flatly. "This was all a mistake."

He looked so agitated I sighed. "You're too cute to stay mad at. Besides, I can see why you wanted to rattle your mother. She's a sniper with those insults. I'm still angry, but at your mother, not at you. She's elitist as hell."

Grant was pacing. "This is the worst guest room, by the way. It's a dig at me."

I thought the room was just about the size of a small nation, but what did I know? In the Caldwell world, posh furnishings and an en-suite bathroom with a copper tub were just bullshit they had to endure. It must be damn hard to be rich. Not.

"So don't let it get to you. Let's just stay and do whatever we want. Say whatever we want. They clearly do. Your grandmother is smoking a Virginia Slim inside and calling relatives sluts. I mean, I think that gives us a free pass to behave however we want."

Grant laughed. "Wait until the rest of the family gets here tomorrow."

"I can't wait," I said dryly. "But if we're staying, I'm serious about going swimming. You owe me a Dirty Dancing moment."

He eyed me, his shoulders relaxing, a smile turning up the corner of his mouth. "I can't possibly deny you that."

"Besides, if we stay and talk about our wedding the entire time, it will make your mother lose her mind. That could be fun."

Grant's gaze dropped to my lips. "I'll make it up to you," he said. "Whatever you want, you can have."

Oh, the possibilities. "I wouldn't offer me carte blanche if I were you. I have a lot of needs." I wrapped my arms around his neck and pressed all that Prada up against his hard chest and thighs. "Most of them involving food or being in bed with you."

Grant brushed his lips over mine. "Like I said. Whatever you want. I owe you at least a hundred orgasms and a private island for doing this."

"Can I have the hundred orgasms on the private island?" That wouldn't be the worst thing to ever happen to me.

"Of course. We can take a private jet and have a butler bring us meals in between orgasms."

If only he were serious. "Perfect. I didn't bring a swimsuit, by the way."

"Check the smallest bag. I ordered one for you. I find you easy to predict."

I found him easy to fall in love with. "I'm doing a terrible job of punishing you for springing the fake engagement on me."

"Agreed. You only play the femme fatale." He eased my jacket off my shoulders. "But I have no complaints. Now let me help you get changed."

"This feels like a trap."

"It's absolutely a trap. One in which I try to convince you that there is no reason we can't have sex right now."

"I can think of a reason," I said, even as he teased over my sweater with his thumbs, finding my nipples.

"What's that?"

I stepped back. "I'm not wearing my slippers." I gave Grant a saucy grin. "Now find me that swimsuit."

I wanted to have sex with Grant, without question.

And while punishing him was essentially punishing myself, I couldn't give him everything. Not all at once. I'd already crumpled like a tissue when confronted with his rationale for the fake engagement.

Grant groaned. "I hate myself for buying those damn things."

"Don't be upset with yourself. It was a shining moment of your thoughtfulness, proving you miles above your family in character and content."

"You *are* the wisest woman in the world," he said.

CHAPTER 12

I wouldn't have thought it would be possible to have my mood turn around after our first hour at the house. But Leah managed to have me grinning in the pool in no time at all. She kept trying to jump up into my arms but just kept managing to collide with my chest and knocking us both back into the water.

We were soaking wet, my beard dripping and her hair clinging to her cheeks and shoulders, but I couldn't stop laughing. "Leah, don't jump *at* me."

"That's how it's done!" she insisted. "I've seen Dirty Dancing three hundred and eleven times. At least."

"But we're in a pool, not on a dance floor. There is physics involved, you know."

"How would I know that? I flunked physics in high school. Anything involving math and science is not my jam."

"Then trust me when I say that you have to let me lift you first, then you can reach forward." She was bouncing on the balls of her feet impatiently, looking more adorable in the red bikini I'd gotten her than anyone had a right to be.

"Fine. We'll do it your way." She shoved her hair back and lifted her arms in the air. "Let's do this thing."

"Awesome. On the count of three."

Leah jumped. She fell back down with a splash.

I waited until she was done spluttering. "I said on the count of three. Which means you have to wait until I actually start counting. You're really terrible at following directions."

"Directions are like contracts. No one really needs them."

"You're killing me. I might actually die listening to you say something so horrifying. Look at me in my final moments before I have a heart attack."

"Okay, drama queen," she said with an eyeroll and a grin. "Your mother's son, I see."

Oh, no, she didn't. "Hey! Bad Leah. Very, very bad Leah." I picked her up around the waist.

She let out a shriek. "Let me go!"

I tossed her through the air. She hit like a mortar. Water went everywhere and she sank.

She came up sputtering, shoving her hair off her face. "What the hell?"

"You said let you go. I let you go." I gave her a smug smile.

Leah splashed me. I splashed her back.

She shrieked and splashed me again, all while backing up.

But I had the advantage of height and larger hands. I splashed in rapid succession until there was almost a constant wave of water hitting her in the face.

Finally, she screamed, "Stop! I give up!"

I stopped. She wasn't mad, she was laughing so hard she could barely breathe. She was soaked, blinking and wiping her face.

"You suck, Grant Edward Caldwell the third."

"You started it. Calling me my mother was fighting words." I walked through the water to her and helped her wipe her face and push her hair back. "You look cute."

"Don't make fun of me."

"I'm not." I bent down and kissed her, tenderly. "I find you cute. Adorable. Beautiful. Sexy. Delicious."

Leah put her hands on my waist and kissed me back. "You can be very sweet, did you know that? In between times when you suck."

That made me laugh softly. "That sounds about right." Leah would never falsely flatter me, that was for sure. I thought of other women I'd dated, who'd blown smoke up the rich guy's ass and knew there was zero comparison with Leah. My money didn't impress her.

"Let's try the lift again. We have to get this right for our wedding." Leah gave me a smirk.

"It's going to be a fantastic wedding, that's for damn sure. I want hot air balloon rides." It wasn't going to happen, so I could have whatever I would want.

She raised her eyebrows. "It's a wedding, not a circus."

"Isn't a wedding a circus?"

"Solid point. Then I want a cotton candy machine."

"That's easy. I also want food trucks. One, because I like tacos. Two, because it will drive my mother insane." We were talking about it like it was real, but it wasn't so it was actually very freeing. I had never once given any thought to what I would want at a wedding, because I was never planning to get married, but it was ironic how readily ideas were coming to me.

"How about a signature cocktail called the Greah? It's our names put together."

"That sounds unappealing as hell, but if you want it, go for it."

"Well, the other option is the Lant, and that sounds even worse."

"That is worse. How about a signature cocktail that is something about us, not our names? Like The Purple Slipper for yours and Tall, Dark, and Handsome for mine."

Leah rolled her eyes. "More like Poodle Skirt for me and The Pancake for you."

"Uh, no. I heartily endorse Poodle Skirt for yours but I veto The Pancake for me. I want to sound more badass than that."

"How about The Bad Boy?"

"That makes me sound seventeen."

"You're very picky."

"I am." I ran my finger over her bottom lip, feelings of possessiveness rising strong and sure. "That's why I chose you."

Her eyelashes swept down, in a move that wasn't what I expected from Leah. "Grant," she murmured.

"What?" I tipped her chin up, forcing her to look at me.

"It's not real," she said, her voice a whisper, her eyes filled with something that made me know she was my future.

She felt it too. It was there in her dark eyes.

Willpower be damned. She'd taken mine and shattered it.

"Leah. It's *real*. You know it is. I know it is."

"What are you talking about?" she asked. "What's real?"

"You. Me." I pulled her closer against me in the pool, the room silent except for the hum of the filter and Leah's nervous breathing. "What's happening between us. It's real and I want to be with you. Date you. Spend time with you. Love you."

She sucked in a breath. "You do? But..."

"But what?"

"I have no idea what I was going to say. I'm freaking out."

"In a good way or a bad way?"

"I think it's good," she said. "Because I really, really like you, even if you are bossy and picky."

That made me laugh softly. She was perfect for me, because she would never let my ego run rampant. "You're impulsive and irresponsible with legal contracts, and I still really, really like you."

Leah looked like she was going to say something.

But I didn't want to hear anything practical or any doubts or fears or concerns.

I didn't want anything to shut down the possibility that we could work.

So I just lifted her up out of the water by the waist. "Lift your legs."

She did, then her arms and screamed, "We're doing it! We're

awesome!"

Then she shifted too far forward. I lost my balance and she went pitching forward. We collided and went under the water.

When we both reemerged, she was laughing and I was shaking my head.

"And this is why I didn't want to do this on marble flooring."

"Good call." She bounced up and down. "Let's get out. I'm wrinkling up."

"That's probably a good idea. We need to get ready for dinner."

"Great. I can't wait to tell your mom about our carnival-themed wedding. She's going to hate it." Leah pulled herself out of the pool and sat down, feet still in the water.

I put my hands on her knees and eased them apart so I could get closer to her. "I can't wait," I said. "For everything." I kissed her.

Leah sighed in pleasure and gave me a mischievous look. "What if this is in the contract and I don't know because I never read it? Like a 'What's real is fake and what's fake is real' mind-meld clause?"

I was the last person in the world who would include a "mind-meld" clause. "Read it and find out."

She wrinkled her nose. "Nah, I'm good."

"Besides, if it's real, how can it be fake?"

For a second I thought she was going to say something snarky, but Leah just ran her fingers through my beard and stared up at me thoughtfully. "It can't be fake."

"No. It can't."

I was drinking more wine than I should.

But dinner with Grant's family was surreal.

Grant saying he had feelings for me was surreal. I had been shocked when he'd said he wanted something real with me, but I'd been ecstatic because the crush developed over pancakes had morphed into a true, deep affection for Grant as I had gotten to know him.

I was in love with him. For real.

That was some seriously surreal, crazy, and probably totally insane stuff.

Staying in a mansion with an indoor pool was surreal.

Even the tartare was surreal. It was a little tiny plate of heaven.

But the conversation among the Caldwells was rapid-fire insults, complaints, gossip, and accusations.

Grant's grandmother lit a cigarette at the table.

His father said, "Mother, you can't do that in here." "Why not?" she asked, crankily, blowing smoke in his direction.

"Because it's not 1977." He pushed his chair back. "Come on, I'll take you outside on the back patio."

"It's freezing out there."

"It's sixty degrees. You'll be fine." He pulled her chair back. "Leah, why don't you join us? You can bring your wine."

I froze, startled to be singled out. My glass was halfway to my lips. I had changed into another stunning outfit, this one the all winter-white Chanel, and I had ordered chardonnay on sheer terror that I might spill. Grant's mother had informed me white wine with beef was tacky, but I'd just used it as an opportunity to tell her about the frozen rosé machine I wanted for the wedding. That had clammed her right up.

But now Grant the second wanted me to go outside and that felt slightly threatening. I looked to my Grant for a cue on how to proceed.

Yep. My Grant. I said it.

He nodded, like he was certain I wouldn't be murdered by his father or permanently disfigured. To be honest, his father definitely seemed easy to deal with. Chill. Casual. Unconcerned.

"Sure," I said, because what the hell else was I going to say? I stood up and did in fact take my wine with me.

Grant's father had his highball glass, no question about that.

He guided Gigi and me to the back patio, where he ensconced her in front of an outdoor gas fireplace. He called a staff member over to turn it on and tipped the guy. Then he lit his mother's cigarette and gestured for me to go around the other side of the double-sided fireplace.

"I can't take the smell of cigarettes anymore," he explained. "Funny thing is I smoked for forty years."

I made a noncommittal sound, wondering why I had to be out there.

He took a sip of his drink and gave me a smile. "You and Eddie aren't really engaged, are you? I saw your face when he dropped that bombshell. You were shocked. Plus, you don't have a ring on your finger."

Which was precisely why I had told Grant not to spring anything on me. My reaction time had been too slow. Damn. Maybe I needed more improv classes.

"It was spontaneous," I said. "There wasn't time for a ring."

"I'm not buying that," he said. "I can see that you care about my son, but as of right now, you have no plans to marry him."

That would be annoyingly accurate. How did the pickled Grant the second ascertain that? Was he secretly in possession of a psychology degree?

"So, what is holding you back?" Grant the second asked me.

"What do you mean?"

"You're holding back from committing to Eddie." He leaned against the stone fireplace, crossed his ankles, and took a sip of his cocktail. Or rather, his glass of gin. "What are you afraid of?"

I wasn't sure how to answer that. I was holding back, but he wasn't supposed to be able to see that. My acting skills definitely weren't up to snuff this weekend. Maybe because I was, you know, busy falling in love with Grant for real.

So the problem was, I didn't want to give that away. But I couldn't give away that this had all started out as a contract, whose terms I didn't read.

Which made me wonder how that worked. Was I still getting paid for this weekend? We had really muddied the water. And by muddied I meant "had dropped an entire oil tanker into a river" kind of muddy.

"Don't be scared to share with me," Grant the second said. "I drink a lot. I probably won't remember half of what you say."

Somehow, I doubted that. He was using alcohol as a smokescreen so no one would see how astute he really was. I was starting to wonder if the bottle he drank from at the house even had gin in it or if it was just water.

I decided a portion of the truth would ring with sincerity. "I don't want to lose my independence. I want to be a singer and I want to achieve my own level of success. I don't want to give up a career. I would always wonder what if."

"But wouldn't financial freedom allow you to pursue your passions without worrying about paying the rent? Eddie isn't the kind of man to hold it over you, you know."

"Why did it matter to you that Grant has a relationship?" I asked, genuinely curious, thinking about the ultimatum that had started this whole chain of events. "Grant seemed happy with his life the way it was when he and I met. Our relationship was kind of an accident of circumstance. I don't think he was looking for anything."

"I know no one really understands my relationship with Tiff, and yes, we've had our share of drama. But I've spent my whole adult life with her and I wouldn't have it any other way. It's a love I can count on."

I had a feeling Grant, the son, would disagree that Tiffany was reliable but I wasn't going to argue with his father. I mean, hey, if he was happy that was what mattered, right? I just nodded, unsure of what to say. *Your wife seems as loving as a great white shark* didn't really seem appropriate.

"I don't want my son to spend his life alone, in pursuit of financial success or accolades. What does any of that mean in the end? I know Eddie thinks I'm something of a screwup," Grant the second said. "But I made a choice in life. I didn't need to 'increase the empire.' My father made enough money to last for generations. All I have to do is make sure it perpetuates, not necessarily gets larger. So I chose to buy a basketball team and be part of a team of management. It's profitable and I get to spend my days and nights hanging out around a sport I love. What's wrong with that, right?"

That made a whole lot of sense to me. "I think that's fantastic that you get to do what you love." If you could get it, go for it. That was my feeling on that. Wealth had given Grant the second options most people didn't have.

I had to wonder if Grant the second did anything for charitable causes or contributed to the world in any way, but I wasn't about to ask him.

"So why can't you? Eddie can give you that—the opportunity to do what you want."

His father's words made my throat tighten. "Because that's the problem. I don't want anyone to give it to me. I want to do it on my own."

"Say you had a friend who said, 'Leah, I know the producer for a record label and I can send him your demo.' Wouldn't you jump on that chance? It's called an opportunity."

"It's just different." I wanted out of this conversation. I didn't actually mind Grant's father and he didn't seem like he had ill intentions but he'd never been anything but wealthy. He didn't seem to understand why it mattered to me to take care of myself, especially after eight years of busting my butt in the city. "I don't need anyone to pay my rent. I've been paying it on my own just fine for years."

Grant's father was giving me very real anxiety and I wasn't even sure why. It wasn't like he was being a jerk. He was just being opinionated, which wasn't shocking for a man who'd had everything he ever wanted. Of course, he assumed he was right.

But I felt an intense panic rising inside my chest. It felt like serious indigestion coupled with an inability to breathe. I took a massive sip of my wine.

I'd spent the afternoon feeling like I'd scored a huge win. The fake relationship wasn't really fake and that was exactly what I wanted, whether I had been able to admit it to myself or not.

Now this conversation had me terrified that I was plunging witlessly into a disaster. I didn't belong in this world. It was an act. I was playing the part of rich girlfriend. I couldn't really be a rich girlfriend, could I? Certainly not a wife.

"I don't see how it's different, but okay, I'll stop pressing. I didn't mean to upset you. I just met you, Leah, and I already like you. You've got something special about you."

"Thank you." I wasn't sure what else to say.

"Last thing I'll say is if you really plan to get married, you should elope somewhere. Weddings are a pain in the ass." He pushed off the stones and stood up, the ice in his glass clinking.

Said the man who was throwing himself a three hundred grand anniversary party.

I shivered, despite the wool coat I was wearing. I shifted around to the other side of the fireplace, hoping that Grant's grandmother hadn't heard a word we'd said. She didn't appear to be listening at all. She had a massive ash hovering in the air over her cashmere coat in such a dangerous way I wanted to slid my palm under it and catch it. Save the cashmere. Reading glasses with the lenses the size of dinner plates were on her nose and she was studying her phone.

"Do you think I can get a flight to Paris tomorrow?" she asked.

"Tomorrow is my anniversary party, Mother. You can't go to Paris."

Gigi rolled her eyes and took a hit off of her cigarette. "Paris sounds more entertaining." She studied me with narrowed eyes. "Do you smoke?"

"No."

"That's a shame."

That almost made me laugh.

"Sit with me anyway. Grant, go away. I want to talk to Eddie's girlfriend."

Oh, fabulous. Just exactly what I wanted. Time alone with the slut-shaming grandmother. I was tempted to grab Grant the second's arm and beg him not to leave me alone, but I was serious when I told Grant I'd faced down some serious assholes over the years in the industry. I had thick skin.

"Sure," I said easily and sat down on the stone wall next to her.

Grant's father didn't protest. He just disappeared back into the restaurant.

She ashed her cigarette onto the paver stones. Ashes wafted onto her pants but she either didn't notice or didn't care. "What was your name again, dear?"

"Leah."

"And you're a waitress?"

I nodded. "Yes. And aspiring singer."

"Eddie showed me the video of you singing. You have a lovely voice."

"Thank you." When had Grant done that? Maybe while I'd been in the shower after the pool.

"I shared it for you."

Huh. What did she mean by that? As in she had social media accounts? I guess Gigi was more in tune with modern living than I would have expected. "That was nice of you, thank you."

"I want Eddie to be happy. Tiffany was a terrible mother. I never wanted my son to marry her. I think Eddie is smart to pick an ordinary girl like you. You aren't spoiled."

She had a fair point, but she should probably keep her thoughts about my ordinariness to herself. It was a wee bit insulting. But if I expected anyone to keep a thought to themselves, I was in the wrong crowd. Clearly.

"I am not spoiled, that is true. At the same time, I haven't exactly suffered either. I had a good childhood thanks to my parents and I've managed to make a life for myself in the city." Which I couldn't wait to get back to, to be honest. The fresh air couldn't make up for the eye-rolling factor of the Caldwells.

Grant appeared, looking like he wanted to kidnap me. I wouldn't have objected. "Is everything okay out here?" he asked.

I gave him a reassuring smile. "We're fine."

"Just girl talk, Eddie. Mind your own business." Gigi tossed her cigarette on the ground and put it out with the heel of her boot. "We're going back in now so calm your tits."

I was so startled I laughed out loud before slapping my hand over my mouth.

Grant looked less amused than me.

Gigi stood up and looped her arm through mine. "I could grow fond of you."

"I'm pretty irresistible," I said cheerfully.

Grant laughed and put his hand on the small of my back. "I'll attest to that."

When we got inside, Grant the second was paying the bill. "You kids can stay if you'd like," he said. "But Tiff has a migraine."

Grant's mother was lying face-first on the table. I was pretty sure she was drunk given I'd seen her have three vodka sodas and eat absolutely nothing. It was safe to say she probably needed inpatient treatment but I wasn't about to suggest that to people who seemed to think this was totally acceptable. Part of me felt sorry for Grant's mother, despite how rude she'd been to me. This was not a happy woman, and frankly, that was sad as hell.

"Do you want to stay?" Grant said.

I nodded. "Sure." A perfectly acceptable excuse to spend time alone without his family there? Sold. "I could go for dessert and coffee."

When we were alone and the waiter appeared to clean the various dirty dishes, Grant asked him, "Do you have key lime pie?"

My insides squeezed. He'd remembered. I'd told him it was my favorite dessert and he had remembered. The man was a dream.

"No, sir, I'm sorry, we don't."

"Does anywhere in town have it?"

"I can ask Chef." The waiter scraped crumbs. "If there is, would you like a slice?"

"Yes, two, please." Grant handed the waiter two hundred-dollar bills. "And espresso for the lady."

"Yes, sir."

I liked key lime pie, but I wasn't sure I liked it two hundred dollars' worth. But I wasn't going to complain when Grant was being sweet. I had a feeling he was trying to compensate for his family.

"Someone wants to get lucky tonight," I said with a small smile.

"That's the plan," he told me. "Plus, I need to distract you in whatever way I can from the fact that my family is insane."

"I think I'm a hit with your father and Gigi. I don't think your grandfather has an opinion about me. Your mom hates me."

"My mother hates everyone. I'd be scared if she *did* like you. That would be a clue for me to run far away from you."

"That's a solid point." We were seated at the end of the table, so we were partially facing each other. I turned my chair a little so I could see him even more directly. "How do we do this?" I asked him softly. "What are we actually doing, Grant?"

He reached over and took my hand. "We're getting to know each other even better than we already have. We're going to go back to the city and we're going to spend time together, falling in love. The way people do."

For a man who had sworn he wasn't ever going to get married, he was very confident about this being an easy transition to us having a relationship. I wasn't so sure. "Just like that, huh?"

"Just like that." He adjusted his tie. "Though don't worry, I'll still give you the agreed-on amount for this weekend. I won't negate our contract."

"You and your legal talk. So sexy. Not." Though I had to admit I was relieved about the money because I had taken additional days off work to be here. Without the money promised, rent next month would be tricky.

"I'm being straightforward. I don't want you to worry."

"I appreciate that. But per that contract, this is a sex-free weekend."

"I added an addendum."

I laughed. "What? When?"

Grant grinned, his expression smug and naughty as sin. "After you said you don't read contracts."

I gaped at me. "You rotten bastard."

"It merely states if you change your mind, you are most welcome to get naked with me. I have no objections."

"You're making that up."

"No, I'm not." He held his hands up. "I swear. You really should read documents, Leah."

I would have ripped him a new one except the waiter appeared with my espresso. "The key lime pie is being delivered, Mr. Caldwell. It should be here shortly."

"Thanks, I appreciate it," Grant said, without even looking at the waiter. He was staring at me.

"Thank you," I said to the waiter, embarrassed. Not only was Grant being mildly dismissive of the waiter, he looked like he wanted me to be dessert.

I sipped my coffee after the waiter disappeared. "Stop looking at me like that," I admonished. "We're still in public."

"You don't strike me as a woman who is that shy."

Damn it. He had me there. "Have you had the key lime pie at Blue Heaven in Key West? It's the best thing ever. I was there five years ago and I remember it like it was yesterday."

He shook his head. "I've never been there. Do you want to go next weekend?"

"Sure," I said, joking, because that's the way my world worked. Anyone saying that would be joking. Then I realized he was serious. "What? No. I have to work."

He shrugged. "Another time, then."

That made me uneasy, though I wasn't sure why.

The pie appeared in front of us and I picked up the clean fork the waiter had brought, grateful for a distraction. "This is the best gift you've ever given me," I said, putting a bite into my mouth and closing my eyes. "Mm." I opened my eyes again. "Though the vibrator was thoughtful, I have to admit, but since it wasn't even your idea, it doesn't count."

Grant didn't look at all that interested in the dessert. He hadn't even picked up his fork. "Have you used that vibrator?" he asked, his voice low and rough.

I paused, his tone turning me on. I felt the force of his words all the way to my inner thighs and the memory flared up of me pleasuring myself, his name on my lips, maybe once or twice after we'd flirted on FaceTime. Okay, three times. "I can neither confirm nor deny."

Grant sat back with a groan. "You're killing me."

"Let's say the gesture didn't go unappreciated," I said with a smile.

"Are you done with that pie yet? Because we need to get home."

I shook my head and slowly, painstakingly slid my fork through the pie. "Nope. Not even close." I licked the very tip of the fork in as suggestive a way as I could manage.

"You clearly want my hand on your ass later, don't you?"

Yep. Instant nipple hardening. "What did I do?" I asked, feigning innocence. "I'm just eating my pie."

Grant smiled in a way that made me want to forget the dessert and go straight to the nearest mattress. Hell, the nearest wall. Or this table would do.

"Finish your dessert," he said. "Then I'll have mine."

I ate two more bites like a squirrel pouching nuts. Shove, tuck, chew. "I think I'm full."

I didn't need the calories anyway.

What I did need was Grant.

CHAPTER 13

Not wanting to encounter any of my family, I brought Leah into the house through the garage and up the back stairs.

"I need a tour of this house tomorrow so I can get the lay of the land. I'm afraid I'm going to get lost."

I put my finger to my lips as we moved down the hallway upstairs. "Shh. Don't wake the crazy people." Dinner had been endless, and then Leah and I had hung out. It was after eleven so I had high hopes everyone was fast asleep in anticipation of the next day's party.

Leah gave a soft laugh.

Did she have any idea what that sound did to me? That for six months I'd been listening to that sound and slowly, steadily, growing addicted to it. That now, after two short weeks of spending time with her and talking to her, that laugh had me by the balls.

She was mine. The woman who had made me toss aside

everything I'd ever thought about my future and go all in.

When we got to the north bedroom, I pulled her inside and locked the door behind us. I touched the switch on the wall that handled all the lights and turned just one lamp on low. I wanted to see Leah but without blinding either of us.

I kicked my shoes off and pulled her up against me. "Do you know that you came along and wrecked all of my plans?"

"That sounds like a country song."

"It's the truth. I've spent six months resisting you and then I just fell off a fucking cliff." I brushed her hair back, stunned at how much I loved her. How much just being near her made me happy. How there was no fear or anger that it might all go to shit or wind up dysfunctional.

"For the man who told me he's been accused of holding back emotionally, I have to say I don't know what you're talking about. You seem to know what you want."

I nodded. "I do. I want you. Here, now. Tomorrow. The day after that. And the day after that." For the rest of my life.

"This is crazy, Grant," she murmured. "Isn't this crazy?"

"This isn't crazy. Crazy is my family. We're not crazy." I eased her sweater down off of her shoulders and removed it.

I was going to toss it on the floor but Leah grabbed it. "Don't just throw that around. It was expensive."

That amused me, since I was the one who had paid for it, but I let her take it and set it on the bench at the foot of the bed. I undid the first button on her soft shirt, and then the second. The edge of her bra appeared and I ran my finger across the seam, and the swell of her breast. I couldn't get enough of her body. Leah sighed and pushed her hair back off of her shoulders.

"Take your jacket off," she said. "It's my turn to undo some buttons."

I was wearing a sport jacket with matching pants and a white shirt without a tie. "Be my guest." I shrugged out of my jacket and tossed it on top of hers. I turned back and raised my hands. "I won't stop you."

Lea gave me a smirk. "You don't exactly seem like a submissive guy."

"Not even fucking close. I'm choosing to give you what you want."

She undid the top bottom. "That's my boss man. Totally in charge." She flicked open another button.

I pulled the shirt out of my pants and then reached out to undo another of her buttons. Our speed increased but my fingers fumbled with the small delicate ivory buttons. "I'm tempted to just rip this shirt off of you."

"Don't you dare. This shirt is too beautiful to destroy."

"I like it better when you're in a sweatshirt and leggings. You don't object to my roughness."

"Shh, don't be a brat." She had my shirt undone fully and pulled it apart, slipping her hands inside and running them over my chest.

"A brat, huh?" I took her hands and pulled them down. "My turn."

Her breath caught and she bit her bottom lip in a way that had my cock hardening instantly. And she knew it would.

I finished undoing the final button and slipped her shirt off. She had on an ivory lace bra that showed off her tits to total perfection. Cupping them both, I teased my thumbs over her nipple. I loved that sound she made—a hitching of her breath whenever I made initial contact with her body. She was comfortable in her skin and her confidence was such a huge turn-on.

I studied the smoothness of her flesh, rising above the lace, as I worked the taut buds. In the lamplight her skin glowed, and I found a birthmark I'd never noticed before where her shoulder rounded to the graceful length of her neck. It was a little mocha-colored patch and I flicked my tongue over it, wanting to know every inch of her. Taste everything. Her fingers were looped into my belt, and tightened as I kissed up over her clavicle bone and into the hollow of her neck. I could feel the pulsing of her vein, and hear the shallowness of her breathing close to my ear.

Everything had changed.

Everything.

My life, my future. My understanding of who I was and what I wanted.

The intimacy of being with her was foreign, but it took my breath away. I brushed her hair back off her shoulder, sweeping from her temple down to the ends. Her dark eyes were wide, open, caring. I wanted to tell her that I loved her, but the words caught in my throat, choking me. I didn't want to ruin the moment in any way and those were words I hadn't spoken to a single living soul in a decade.

I didn't want them to ring hollow or scare her.

"I want you," I murmured, my voice rough.

"I want you too," she whispered and I knew she meant more than sex, just like I did.

How had a pair of brown eyes and a poodle skirt torn down the façade of my life and exposed me to everything I had been missing?

I didn't know and truthfully didn't care. I eased her bra straps down off of her shoulders and followed the path with my lips, undoing the clasp on her back at the same time. Her bra slipped down between us, caught by my belt buckle, exposing her breasts to me. Leah was all natural. I took my time tasting her, teasing her, enjoying every little hitch of breath and sigh of pleasure she gave.

When I undid her pants, she shifted her hips back to let the bra fall to the floor. She let go of my belt loops and ran her hands over my chest. I didn't even consider speaking. There was nothing to say that would be right or enough or important without shattering the deep growing bond between us. I used my lips to brush along her jaw, the corners of her mouth, the delicate skin at the peak between her cheek and her eye, holding her while I did, hands gliding over her abdomen, the small of her back, up to her shoulder blades.

I lost any sense of time. There was just me and Leah and a hushed room.

When I eased down her zipper, the pants gave in to gravity and dropped. She stepped out of them and I divested myself of my white shirt. Not wanting her to worry about the damn clothes, I just bent and picked up the pants. I folded them while drawing her bottom lip into my mouth. She gave a soft gasp that had me hard as steel.

I set them on the bench at the foot of the bed, then removed my own pants. I just tossed them behind me, not giving a fuck. When I turned back, she had sat down on the bench and was reaching for the waistband of my boxer briefs. For half a second I debated taking her and tossing her on the bed, not wanting to lose the upper hand on my control, but then she pulled my cock out. I decided I wanted to see her mouth wrapped around me more than I wanted to direct every move.

Leah was running her hand over the smooth flesh with one hand and shoving down my briefs with the other. She gazed up at me and it was the sexiest expression I had ever seen. She looked vulnerable and beautiful and... *devoted* to me.

I gripped the sides of her head, burying my fingers in her hair, and I guided her down onto me, wanting to test myself, see how long I could let her suck. The slickness of her tongue eased down my cock and I gritted my teeth, knowing this was going to be torture.

Knowing I was going to love every fucking second of it.

I had a mouth full of Grant and I had never felt more powerful in my entire life. It had been impulse to sit down, but now I loved that I had. He was gripping my hair so hard, the strands tugged at the roots, pain occasionally flaring, and he was completely silent. Which told me he was using every shred of self-control to stay that way. Like he didn't trust himself not to explode.

Enclosing his shaft with my hand, I took the full length of him over and over, as his hard cock grew slicker and slicker. He was so hard I had to work to open myself for him, and I could feel the unleashed power behind him. His thighs were clenched, his grip growing tighter with each pass. He wanted to drive his cock into my mouth, that was clear. Take over. Get dirty and rough and possessive. Part of me wanted to let him. Part of me wanted to use this to hold him just slightly away from me before we both fell head over ass into something neither one of us could predict would work.

It was scary as hell.

Which is why I didn't want to look into his eyes. Those stunning green eyes that had known a lifetime of reserve, and not much love.

Because I loved him and I was afraid for him to see that.

I wanted this. Him and me and hot, sexy nights.

Forever.

That's when I knew that he needed to let go, just as much as I did.

Nostrils flaring, I pulled back. I stared up the length of his muscular chest. "Would it be crazy if I said that I'm falling in love with you?" I whispered, going for broke. Maybe that made me ordinary, as Gigi has called me.

Maybe it made me stupid.

But I was always a woman who went for what she wanted.

Grant said it was real and I believed him.

He tensed and his grip on my hair loosened. He shook his head slowly. "Not crazy at all. Because I'm falling in love with you too."

He pulled me to my feet, our warm skin brushing close. Grant's gaze met mine and he cupped my cheeks, kissing me softly. With a tenderness that made me want to cry.

"Leah, Leah, and Leah," he said.

I laughed softly. "That's my name."

But he shook his head. "That's not what I mean. *Leah*. My favorite in any category."

My heart squeezed. "I feel the same way."

"Actually," he said. "There are no categories. There's only you."

I might as well have melted. That's the way I felt. No longer flesh, no longer bone. Just liquid and spilling over outside of myself. Without any thought from me a sound came out of my mouth, one of passion and desperation, that had Grant lifting me up by the hips and wrapping me around his legs.

We kissed with tangled tongues and hot pants of love and desperation. He gripped my ass and I clung to his neck. I had my panties on still and I rose up and down, urgently grinding against his cock, wanting more, wanting everything. My nipples brushed against his hard chest, goose bumps racing down my arms.

Grant tore aside the scrap of lace that was my panties and rocked up into me with a surge that had me gasping for air. All that hot hard cock deep inside my wet and welcoming body was everything I could ever want. He took me fast, urgently, and I held his shoulders, head back, soft cries escaping before I could stop them.

My orgasm had me clawing at Grant with my fingernails, voice rising on a careening moan of sheer pleasure. My inner walls held on to him, and I was shocked at the power of it. Before I could recover, Grant dropped me on the bed without breaking our connection. He started to move inside me again, one palm next to my head, eyes boring into mine.

Emotion swelled up in my chest and I felt like I could cry. My body was on fire with passion, another orgasm swelling on the heels of the first, and my heart was overwhelmed.

"I love you," he said.

Any sense of holding back shattered with those words. He wasn't falling in love. He was saying he loved me.

My instinct was to close my eyelids against the intensity of Grant, but I didn't want to do that. I wanted to see what was in his pale green eyes and remember this forever.

"I love you, too," I said, lifting my hips to meet him.

Grant kept his eyes locked on mine as he exploded inside me.

He collapsed onto me and we lay there, stunned, hot, intertwined.

Neither of us moved. Neither of us spoke.

Sometimes you just need to stay silent and let the moment ride.

We fell asleep that way, his heavy weight and warm breath cocooning me.

"You're going where?" I gaped at Grant, still concentrating on prying my eyes open. "And why wasn't I invited?"

"Golfing. We'll be back by two."

Um, what the actual fuck? I hadn't expected him to hold my hand all day but one, his family was nuts. Two, he'd told me he loved me the night before. Didn't that count for at least one day of kissing and adoring gazes aimed at me over bagels and lox? "You're seriously leaving me alone here all day? Why can't I go with you?"

"Do you golf?" He looked skeptical and not at all like he was going to miss me.

Was I wrong in thinking he should miss me? It seemed like an appropriate response to you know, love. Like, just-happened love. Holy crap, we had stepped off an emotional cliff together.

"No, I don't golf, but I could learn." I had no opinion about golfing one way or the other. I'd never even thought about it as something I might or might not want to do. But now it suddenly seemed like a hobby I'd adore in comparison to spending the day at Casa Cranky Caldwell. I sat straight up and threw the covers back, ready to get up and get in golfing gear.

"Leah, I don't think it's a good idea. My grandfather has no patience for novice golfers. Trevor and his dad are meeting us too."

"Who is Trevor?"

"My best friend. His dad has a house about ten miles from here. He'll be at the party tonight."

Grant had a best friend? Of course he had a best friend. Most people did. I didn't know as much about Grant as I'd thought I did. "Then I definitely want to go so I can meet Trevor." I stood up and threw my arms around his neck, totally naked, and gave him a kiss, trying to be seductive and persuasive. "Please don't leave me here."

He gave a moan. "Leah. I can't take you. Just hang out with Gigi. She likes you. My mom will be doing her hair and makeup and all that stuff all day. You won't even see her."

Hang out with Gigi. That sounded like a blast. "This whole men go golfing, women do their hair, is very sexist." I could feel my lip pulling into a pout. I shouldn't have fallen asleep so quickly after sex the night before. I'd closed my eyes on a high and woken up to reality.

"I agree, it's very gender-based. But everyone is doing what they personally would prefer to do."

I gave him a look.

"Well. Except for you. I'll take you golfing a different time so you can learn and then in the future I won't leave you behind, I promise."

That was an unnerving thought. If Grant and I were going to be in a real, legitimate relationship, this would not be my only visit to the Hamptons. Yikes.

"That does not help me today."

Grant pulled my arms down and set me away from him. He was wearing a navy sweater and plaid pants. He looked like a model pretending to be a golfer. "I'll make it up to you. I promise."

I'd heard that before. "That promise better involve cake."

"I was thinking sexual favors."

"No, thanks, I'll take cake." I gave him a grin. Hey, sure I would like sexual favors. But didn't he win in that scenario as well? Nope. Not giving him any satisfaction.

"You seem very motivated by sweets."

"Keep that in mind." I yawned and stretched.

"Leah. Put some clothes on before you find yourself on your back." Grant looked turned on and dangerous.

Just the way I liked him.

I strode past him to the bathroom. "Go whack some balls around. I'll see you later." I slammed the door shut.

He knocked on the door.

I opened it a crack. "Yes?"

"Kiss me."

Grant didn't wait for me to respond to his demand. He pressed his lips to mine in the narrow space between the door and frame.

"I love you," he murmured.

All my irritation with him evaporated. How could I be upset when he was staring at me like that and telling me that he loved me?

I couldn't. "I love you, too."

I did. My heart felt ten times larger than normal.

"Leave," I said softly. "Before I kidnap you and keep you forever."

For a second he opened his mouth, then closed it and shook his head with a smile. "See you later."

Unlike Tiffany, I needed to eat, so after showering, I went in search of food. The house was a flurry of activity with the kitchen filled with catering staff. A glance out of the massive glass windows showed tents going up in the yard. There was a rental company unloading tables and chairs. Definitely a spare-no-expense party.

"Good morning," I said to a couple of the women opening large containers and arranging food onto trays. "I'm sorry to be in the way. I just need some kind of quick breakfast."

A woman in her forties with funky glasses smiled at me. "Not a problem. Can I fix something for you? I'm Chef Tamara Walker. I'd shake your hand but I'm wrist-deep in ahi tuna."

"It's nice to meet you. I'm Leah, Grant's fiancée." That just rolled right off the tongue. I should probably question why but not now. I needed coffee. "I'm fine, thanks, I'll just grab something out of the fridge."

I opened the professional subzero refrigerator and was confronted with container after container of food for the party. "Huh." I pried the lid off of one and found a fruit and mint salad. Bingo.

I found a fork and a bowl and dished up a serving. I felt like I was winning until I turned and assessed the coffee machine. "Does anyone know how to use this? I feel like I'm looking at the panel on an airplane."

Gigi wandered into the kitchen. "You shouldn't drink coffee, it'll kill you."

Interesting. She had an unlit cigarette in her hand.

"We have to die from something," I told her.

"That is true." She turned to one of the caterers. "Can you figure this thing out? My future granddaughter needs coffee." She gave me a smile. "What are your plans today?"

"Staying out of the way," I said, truthfully. "There is a lot going on here. I may go for a swim."

Gigi was wearing wide-leg pants and a massive cowl-neck sweater that swallowed her. "We should have flown to Paris last night like I wanted to. We could be shopping right now and still make it back for the party."

I was one hundred percent sure she was serious. I was also one hundred percent sure, if I was one of the caterers, I'd be eavesdropping like nobody's business.

"Paris would have been nice," I said.

"Maybe we can go next weekend."

Sure, right after I got back from Key West. Not going to happen. I had a job and zero flexibility. "I have to work." Even if I didn't, I couldn't exactly picture myself jetting off to Paris with Gigi. I'd prefer my first time there to be, you know, romantic.

"You should quit that waitress job."

"I can't." I didn't want to talk about this. I scooped fruit into my mouth and chewed fast, wanting to escape the kitchen.

Fortunately, Gigi seemed to lose interest when she got a text on her phone. "Oh, I need to answer this."

I bolted for my bedroom and found my own phone. I felt cut off from the world. I had a missed call from my agent, Laura. I called her back.

"Hey, what's up?" Maybe she had an audition opportunity for me.

"Listen, I got a phone call from Ricky Preston."

For a second I was so caught off guard I couldn't process what she'd said. "Ricky Preston, the director?" What the hell did that have to do with me?

"Yes. He wanted your bio and headshot. Apparently, his godmother put your name in his ear. Since when do you know Van Buren Caldwell?"

"Who is Van Buren Caldwell?" I asked, bewildered. "I mean, I'm at the Caldwells' house in the Hamptons right now because I'm dating Grant, but I don't know who Van Buren is." I wasn't sure if that was a man or a woman or a restaurant on the Upper East Side.

"She's Grant's grandmother. Renowned socialite and Broadway enthusiast. She's financed major productions over the years."

"Gigi is Van Buren?" I had no idea. I paced the room. I went over to the window and pulled the drapes back. The view was the driveway. I dropped the drapes again. "I'm so confused."

"She's very influential and so is Ricky Preston, as you know. He wants you to audition to play a young Cher."

"*What*?"

"Yes. I'll send you the details. This is a breakout role. But I guess if you're calling Van Buren Caldwell 'Gigi,' you've got a serious advantage. This is great, Leah."

It was. It was everything I'd ever wanted. Why did it feel so weird? "I don't know what to say."

"Say you're ready. This could be it, kiddo."

This could be it.

And I suddenly felt like I couldn't breathe and my clothes were three sizes too tight.

CHAPTER 14

The house was filling up with people. I'd clapped my hand on men's shoulders and hugged female relatives who had poured in from all over the East Coast. Caterers were already gliding around, though they'd moved their center of operation from the kitchen to a room off the living room designed for that purpose.

I'd been to a million parties growing up. I'd been to a million more as a businessman. As a child, it had been a brilliant opportunity to run around unattended because the watchful Rose wasn't allowed downstairs during events. I had crammed hors d'oeuvres in my mouth by the fistful and stolen sips of champagne, wrinkling my nose at the fizz. Later, I'd gone for the hard stuff, and kisses in dark hallways with girls older than me. As an adult, parties were business opportunities, not social events for me, filled with potential deals and duties to relatives.

This was the first party in years that could bring back the

excitement of being thirteen and impressing my friends by slamming back whiskey.

Because of Leah.

I had every intention of stealing kisses in a dark hallway with Leah, the woman I was in love with. The woman I could not stop thinking about. My grandfather had whacked me upside the back of my head on the golf course, irritated with my level of distraction.

"Get your dick out of the dirt," he'd told me. "Fucking focus. I'm not here to wait around while you jerk off."

He'd been right. I didn't have my head in the game.

Now I had Leah by my side and I felt like I'd scored the biggest deal of my entire life. A woman who could make me laugh and loved me for me. I smiled at her as she accepted yet another hug from a stranger. She stuck her tongue out at me over Aunt Judith's shoulder. I shook my head at her, amused.

When Aunt Judith wandered away in search of a chardonnay, Leah tilted her head and gave me a manic smile as we finally had a minute alone. "Hi, hello, yes, it's so nice to meet you. Pleasure. Charmed. Lovely, isn't it? Oh my, what a fabulous dress. No, I wasn't on the hospital board in Greenwich, but I have that kind of face. Really? That's astonishing. I know, aren't hurricanes ridiculous?"

I grinned. "You do 'the pretty' very well. Even if you're being sarcastic." I flicked my finger over the necklace she was wearing, wishing I could dip lower into the cleavage of the dress. I wanted to pull the fabric forward and drink in the sight of her tits, but I restrained myself. For now. "Have I told you how beautiful you are?"

"Only six times. I'm aiming for an even ten."

She *was* beautiful. The red Valentino hugged her in all the right places and complemented her dark hair. I'd heard her explain to a few people why she was wearing sneakers with it, but most didn't ask. They assumed it was intentional, a middle finger to conventional heels, given that Leah was young. She did look cool, and in command of herself. No one seemed to intimidate her.

Part of me knew she was playing a part. For me.

Part of me hoped she wasn't.

"You're beautiful," I murmured. "That's seven." I was about to coax her to disappear down the hall with me into the library to do dirty things when Max, my developer, appeared at our side.

"Hey, listen," he said, without preamble and not bothering to glance at Leah. "I just got off the phone with Boerger, the head of that arts renewal foundation, and they're letting the theater go. Papers coming over tonight, we'll sign and own it, and then meet with the city to schedule demolition. We already know the Prentiss doesn't qualify for historic preservation so full steam ahead." He clapped my shoulder and turned when he spotted a waiter. "Hey, can I get a vodka tonic?"

Well, fuck. Max had just told Leah what I had intended to tell her on Monday. That I was trying to buy the theater she loved. I straightened my tie and turned. Her face was a mask of confusion and irritation.

"You're tearing down the theater? Why?"

"I own all the land around it. The project has been in the works for a year."

Leah blinked. She was wearing full makeup with false eyelashes and they seemed alien to me, emphasizing how rapidly she was blinking, as if she were holding back tears. "What are you planning to build there?"

I cleared my throat. "Condos. I was going to tell you on Monday. I didn't think this would go through so soon. We've been pressing the foundation for months and gotten nowhere."

"Condos?" she scoffed. "Because that's what the East Village needs more of. Not. Why didn't you tell me when you met me at the theater?"

"Because I wanted you to say yes to this weekend." It was the hard truth. I wasn't going to lie about it. "And like I said, wheels were turning slow on the project anyway."

"I see. So you wanted your way."

Her voice sounded calm, but colder than I would like. I'd known she wouldn't appreciate the theater being torn down, but I hadn't thought she'd see it as anything other than a business deal.

"I wouldn't put it that way."

"How would you put it? You purposely withholding information from me so that I would say yes to you?"

Huh. Good question. "I was controlling the situation. Preventing needless upset if it wasn't necessary. It might have never been relevant." Then I hastened to add again, "Though I was planning to tell you when we got back now that we're... involved." Now that I had told her that I loved her.

Leah nodded, but she was digging her teeth into her bottom lip. "I happen to love that theater."

"I know, and I'm sorry. It's a bad location. Maybe we can buy you another theater. Or you can help me find a way to incorporate some of its elements into the design for the new high-rises. Maybe we have a theater room in one of them." I was just throwing shit out there, spitballing.

She did *not* look happy.

"I'm not a child, Grant. You can't throw me a consolation prize. 'Here's a bike in exchange for having to move to Poughkeepsie.' I don't want a theater. I don't want property. That's not the point."

"What is the point?" I knew what the point was but I was going to plead ignorance and hope it blew over. I had absolutely zero experience with a situation like this. Most women in my life would have taken the consolation prize, used it to their advantage.

"The point is you manipulated me."

That made me frown. "That is an overreaction."

Her eye widened. "Oh, don't tell me how I feel."

"What?" Now I was really confused. "What are you talking about? I'm not telling you how you feel." What the fuck was even happening? I spotted Victoria beelining for us, and was grateful as hell for the interruption. "Can we talk about this later? My cousin is coming over."

Leah gave me a dirty look, spun on her heel, and left me standing there alone.

"Hey, asshole," Victoria said, coming in for a hug. "I heard you're engaged. I call bullshit."

I gave her the obligatory hug, but I was looking over her shoulder to see where Leah was retreating. She disappeared out the glass doors to the patio.

"I am engaged." That was a lie, but it wasn't a total lie in that we were dating.

"Since when?" She pulled back and studied my face. "You haven't said a word about dating anyone special."

"I don't share my personal life, you know that."

A perfectly shaped eyebrow rose. "You are a weirdo that way, that is true. If this is true, which I'm still not convinced of, where is this creature who scored the most eligible bachelor in New York?"

"She went for a drink," I lied easily. I was a little fucking concerned Leah was pissed at me for real.

"Point her out to me."

"She's a brunette in a red Valentino dress wearing white sneakers."

"Intriguing." Victoria glanced around. "I'm off to run her down."

Great. That would thrill Leah.

I turned and almost ran into Trevor. "Hey," I said. "Can you chase Victoria down and make sure she doesn't harass Leah?"

"I'm not your errand boy. Fuck off," Trevor said mildly. "Just me being here stretches the limits of our friendship."

"Fair enough." I eyed my best friend. "Do you think you could stuff your face anymore?" He was holding an appetizer plate loaded eight inches high.

"Food is my cover. If I'm eating, I don't have to talk. Just nod and listen. Nod and listen."

"That is a solid strategy." I glanced over at the patio again. I couldn't see Leah.

"How's the con going?" Trevor asked.

"Okay." Currently, not great. "I'm in love with her."

Trevor choked on a canape. "What the fuck? Are you kidding me? How did that happen?"

"I wish I knew. Man, I'm so fucked." I could admit it to him. "And I don't know what to do."

"Don't look at me." Trevor picked up a scallop. "I don't know anything about women."

I wasn't sure I did either. "I think she's mad at me." I explained about the theater.

"Buy her flowers? Fuck if I know."

I didn't know either and I hated that. I did not like not being in control of a situation and this was no ordinary business deal. This was my future. This was my damn heart, for fuck's sake.

"Don't they say you should do a big gesture?" I asked.

"Who the hell is they? But yeah. That sounds legit."

I had an idea. I straightened my tie. If you want something, go out and get it. That was the Caldwell way. "I gotta go. See you later."

"You're going to do something stupid. I can sense it."

Determined, I stole a scallop off Trevor's overloaded plate and popped it into my mouth. "Never."

Then I went off to find the woman I intended to marry.

Uneasy and not wanting to talk to any of Grant's family, I slipped outside to the patio. No one was out there. It was cold and

I shivered in my cocktail dress, rubbing my arms. The view was amazing. The grasses waved back and forth in the chill autumn breeze and the water was restless, tossing up white caps and hurling them toward the beach.

My feelings were as intense as the ocean. Churning, frothy, dangerous. All of those things.

I was in love with Grant and it was amazing and wonderful and overwhelming.

We'd done this all wrong. We'd complicated everything with contracts and money exchanging hands and expensive gifts.

Did he have a right to withhold information from me?

I didn't know. Maybe he did. At that point he had just wanted to hire me for an acting position.

Except we'd already had sex.

And now? It felt like he should have told me about the theater at some point in all those phone calls and days spent together.

What it told me was that if he wanted something, he was going to get it, even if he had to withhold information.

That was an unnerving thought.

I pulled my phone out of my dress pocket (pockets in a dress are the best thing ever) and saw that I had a text from Savannah.

Your video is BLOWING UP. I'm so happy for you!

Savannah was prone to exaggeration but out of curiosity I went and looked at the Ava Maria video. Suddenly it had over two hundred thousand views. What the hell? I was both thrilled and weirded out.

The second text from Savannah read: *Also. JEALOUS. Look at how hot and cool you look.*

She'd attached a picture of me. I was standing next to Grant in what had turned into a makeshift receiving line. Grant looked every inch the billionaire in his suit, one hand in his pocket, the other holding a crystal cocktail glass filled to the brim with expensive whiskey. I was smiling at a guest, acting the gracious hostess, like I belonged here. The backdrop was the wall of windows with a view of the water beyond. You could see the marble floor and other guests wandering past in designer clothing.

I saw that Savannah had found it on Grant's cousin's social media. The cousin I hadn't even met yet. The caption was: Cuz and his bitch. Aunt Tiff's anniversary party. #happyanniversary #35yearsoffuckingthesameguy. #dontdoit.

Charming. I was "his bitch." I knew she meant it as an attempt at humor but it ticked me off.

My phone buzzed with another text message.

It was from Lou, my manager.

Partying with the rich guy in the Hamptons, huh? You said you were sick. After you taking all those days off with your ankle, sorry, kid, I have to let you go. Did you even really sprain your ankle? That's the same guy who took you home that day.

My heart sank to my gut. Let me go? Was I *fired*?

I had lied about the weekend. I knew I couldn't get more days off, so I had claimed I was sick. How the hell would Lou know I was in the Hamptons?

Fucking social media.

Savannah sent another picture of me and Gigi, arms wrapped

around each other. I did pose for that one. Grant had taken it.

I was all over the damn internet looking like a socialite. A weekend wife. The kind a rich billionaire ignored all week, then trotted out at parties on Saturdays.

I texted my boss back, heart racing. I couldn't lose my job. I'd been there three years and the tips were what kept me afloat.

I'll make it up to you. Please don't fire me. You know I'm a good server.

You used to be reliable. You're not now. Sorry, but this is like a no-call/no-show. My hands are tied.

Frustrated and scared, I shoved my phone back in my pocket. I shivered and turned to stare into the living room of the Caldwells' house.

Maybe I didn't belong here.

The door opened and Grant stood in the doorway, the light behind him keeping his face in shadows. "Are you okay?" he asked. "It's freezing out here."

He started to peel his suit jacket off, clearly to offer it to me. My heart broke a little. He was a kind man. Or tried to be, despite being raised the way he had been.

Maybe we could talk. Maybe we could sort all of this out.

But at the moment all I could feel was a sense of panic that everything was changing and I had no control over any of it. I had lost my job and that terrified me. "I'm coming in. You can keep your jacket on."

When I tried to pass him, Grant wrapped his arms around me in a hug. "Your arms are freezing." He gave me a smile. "And your little cute nose is red."

I couldn't quite meet his gaze, not wanting to explain I'd lost my job. He would tell me it was no big deal. I'd find another one. Or worse, he'd offer to help me out financially, which would make me feel like a failure.

So I wasn't going to tell him.

Which made me no better than him not telling me about the theater.

We both wanted to control the relationship.

There was a pit in my stomach.

"Let's go," he said, releasing me. "They're doing a toast to the illustrious Tiffany and Grant Caldwell. I need you to be there."

"Of course." I stepped inside.

Grant touched my elbow. "Hey. What's wrong?"

Everything. "Nothing." I gave him a smile. "I just got overheated."

How was that for acting skills?

This was not the time or the place to dissect our relationship.

He nodded. We reentered the party and weaved through guests to the massive stone fireplace. Grant's parents were in front of it. His mother looked happy, for once. She was actually smiling. His father did not have a drink in his hand. They were staring at each other, and they did actually look like they were in love. Huh. Fascinating. I guess that was a lesson for me in "mind your own business and don't judge other people."

"I want to raise my glass to my life partner, the incomparable Tiffany Caldwell." Grant's father raised his empty hand, and then made a face. "Why the hell don't I have a drink?"

The room laughed. Tiffany tittered.

Someone scrambled to provide Grant the second with a glass of champagne. "To Tiffany," he said and lifted it.

"To Tiffany," voices repeated and glasses rose.

It was fascinating. As far as I had witnessed and heard, Tiffany was a miserable human being, but here were a hundred people toasting to her. The irony of it was not lost on me.

We all clapped.

Grant dropped my hand and moved to the front of the room. "I'd like to wish my parents a happy anniversary. Thank you for paving the way for me to see how a marriage can and should last."

I almost snorted. I wasn't the only one with acting skills.

His parents looked like they saw nothing other than truth in that statement.

"In the spirit of the day I'd like to announce my own intentions to my amazing and talented girlfriend, Leah." His eyes found mine. "Leah, can you come up here, please?"

The pit in my gut grew. Why the hell was he doing this? It would only piss his mother off and make everyone in his circle believe we actually were engaged. Which we weren't.

But there was a murmur of surprised voices, shifting feet, and curious stares being directed at me and I didn't have a choice. I walked across the room, reminding myself this was a stage. It was an act. A performance. Nothing more.

Play the part. Smile, laugh, repeat.

He held his hand out to me and I took it, using all of my training to prevent a glare from stealing over my features. I didn't want to be put on the spot like this, not after everything we'd shared. Not after we'd blurred every line you could possibly blur.

I could see Tiffany's smile slipping. She was pissed she was no longer the center of attention. Grant was going to regret doing this, that was clear.

But that thought evaporated when Grant went down on one knee.

What the hell?

My heart started to race, and my palms instantly went cold and clammy. My mask slipped a little and I scrambled to comprehend what he was doing.

"Leah," he said. "Will you do me the great honor of becoming my wife?"

My blood froze. He was pulling a ring box out of his pocket. He opened it up to a shockingly large clear-cut diamond ring in a square setting.

He had a ring. Why did he have a ring?

There were excited gasps and a hush of anticipation.

I was supposed to say yes. I was being paid to say yes.

But my throat was constricted and all I could do was nod.

He gave me a wicked, pleased smile, then slid the ring onto my finger.

I burst into tears.

I didn't mean to. But there they were, bursting forth as I felt confused and irritated and in love and wishing it was all real.

But glad it wasn't at the same time.

The reaction genuinely startled Grant, but not the room. Everyone seemed thrilled that a woman would be so happy at a proposal she'd cry. I could hear all their pleased exclamations and someone yelled out, "Never thought I'd see the day!" to which everyone laughed.

Grant the second was nodding in approval but Tiffany looked like she'd swallowed a lemon.

My Grant (damn it, why did that still sound so good?) stood up and pulled me into his arms. He kissed me and I kissed him back because everyone was watching and because I had all kinds of crazy feelings. The ring felt like a boulder resting heavily on my finger.

He pulled back and stared at me and I couldn't read his expression at all. "I love you," he said.

He'd said it right in front of everyone and I wanted to say it back.

But I also wanted to run away like a serial killer was chasing me. Just bolt without looking back. I felt trapped and uncertain what was real and what was fake.

The hours loomed ahead of me. Congratulations. Questions. Stares. Photos.

I did the only thing I could do under the circumstances.

I faked a faint and went down in a heap at Grant's polished Italian shoes.

CHAPTER 15

"What the fuck was *that*?" I asked Leah, running my hands through my hair. She was propped up on our bed but I was still trying to slow my heart rate back down to normal after watching her crumple to the ground.

I had freaked the fuck out, thinking she had really fainted. The room around me had exploded with gasps.

But I knew her well enough that when I dropped down and gathered her into my arms and she "came to" that it was all an act. I had waved off offers to call for an ambulance and had carried her up the stairs.

I heard Aunt Judith say with great authority that Leah was most likely pregnant.

Which had momentarily terrified me before I realized that was unlikely.

No, she had just decided to drop to the floor like a ragdoll.

Leah had kicked off her shoes and was sitting up, cheeks flushed, looking agitated. "What was that? I could ask you the same thing! What the hell was *that*? I was just getting the hell out of there after you blindsided me. *Again*."

"I wanted everyone to know how I feel about you." I had. I did. I had also wanted Leah to understand that I may have fucked up with not telling her about the theater but that my feelings were real.

A grand gesture.

It worked in movies.

"Now everyone is going to think we're engaged!" Leah reached behind her head and unclasped her necklace. She tossed it on the bedside table.

None of this was going according to plan. "We are engaged. You said yes."

She frowned at me. "That wasn't real."

"Yes, it was." So her yes wasn't actually a yes? That did not make me happy.

Her jaw dropped. "That was real? Grant!"

"What?"

"I thought it was an act."

"I gave you a ring." Fucking great. My grand gesture had gone over exactly the opposite of how I had intended. "I had it delivered tonight. I bought it today." It had taken thirty minutes and a massive amount of money but whatever. Clearly, she thought it was all bullshit.

I was pissed and hurt.

At my reminder of the ring, she jerked and tugged it off her finger. She set it next to the necklace. "We can't get married. We just started dating. Why would you even think that?"

It was like being slapped.

I reared back. "Because I'm in love with you."

I had never truly loved a woman. I knew what I knew. What the hell was there to wait for? What would be different in a year or six months? Nothing.

I wanted her.

She looked at a loss as to what to say.

It was there on her face. She didn't want the same thing.

"I don't want to be an impulse, Grant. This is all exciting and new and then what happens in a couple of months? I don't want to be a regret or the woman you see for a couple of hours on the weekend. A rich man's weekend wife."

Wow. That was fucking harsh.

"Then I guess you really don't know me at all, do you? My mistake." That hurt. I had shown her me, without walls up, and she thought I was the kind of guy who just wanted something and took it. I shoved my hands in my pockets. "Are you coming back to the party?"

She shook her head no.

My nostrils flared and my throat constricted. "Fine. I'll tell them you're sick."

"I can't marry you," she said, wrapping her arms over her middle. She looked troubled.

"You don't have to. I'll tell everyone in a week or two we broke up." That would fit right in with her opinion of me.

"Are we breaking up?" she asked, looking like she might cry.

I knew I was being an asshole, but I couldn't help it. It felt like I was being gutted. It felt like I was alone. Again. Like always.

"We were never really together, were we?" I said, and my voice was cold, angry.

Leah winced.

I left the room and returned to the party, going straight for the bar. I poured a whiskey and forced an easy smile onto my face. I turned and spent the rest of the night accepting congratulations and reassuring everyone Leah was fine.

That night I slept in the library on the chesterfield sofa.

In the morning, I left at dawn and sent Leah back to the city with Trevor.

I didn't want to see her.

I couldn't bear to see her.

It would hurt too much.

On Monday I had a check sent to her.

On Tuesday I signed the papers to buy the theater and told Max I didn't want to tear it down.

On Wednesday I went to the diner to apologize because I owed her that. I could handle seeing her in a public place. Maybe. I needed to man up and say I was sorry for leaving her at my parents' house and explain why. That it had hurt like hell and I wasn't used to letting anyone in. That I'd let her fully in, fallen in love, and then fucked it up because I didn't know what I was doing.

I wanted to say all of that and more.

But she wasn't even there.

"She doesn't work here anymore," the hostess told me.

"What?" I frowned at her. Leah had worked there for years. She'd told me that. Would she quit to avoid seeing me? It didn't seem like her style. Leah was a dreamer and an optimist, but she was also practical.

The other server Leah had always worked with eyed me up and down, a stack of dirty dishes in her hand. "She got fired. She called in sick then boss man saw she was partying in the Hamptons with you. She didn't tell you?"

No. She hadn't told me.

I left the diner. Stood on the corner, thought a minute.

Then turned around and went back in.

"What is going on in here?" Felicia said, pounding on my door. "You've been in your room for three days and I'm freaking out that you're spiraling."

Oh. I was spiraling. That was an understatement. "Go away."

"No. I'm coming in."

I hadn't bothered to lock my door because who cared about anything? Not me.

Felicia shoved the door open, flipped on the light, and stepped into my room, wrinkling her nose. I can't say the room was smelling fresh.

I blinked against the harsh light like a baby mole. I'd been in the dark for three days with only my phone for light.

"Oh, hell no," she said, when she saw me. "No, no, and no."

"Leave me alone," I said, clutching the bottle of wine to my chest. The bottle of wine I was holding against the Valentino cocktail dress Grant had bought me, that I was currently wearing while lying in my bed, slippers on my feet.

I took a sip of wine. My hair was a rat's nest and my cheeks were tight from dried tears.

"This is not healthy."

"Of course it's not healthy! It's me having a meltdown. If I were you, I'd look away. It ain't pretty."

"Leah. Give me the wine." She held her hand out and gave me a firm look. "When did you last eat?"

"I'm eating grapes," I said, not interested in relinquishing my bottle.

I was, without question, totally drunk.

I was also broken-hearted and devastated.

Grant didn't come to the north bedroom Saturday night.

And he had Trevor drive me home in the world's most awkward commute back into the city. He'd tried small talk and I had cried. Eventually he'd just turned up the radio and pretended he didn't hear me weeping and sucking snot back up into my nostrils. Considering it was my first meeting with him, I'm sure I left an absolutely fabulous impression. At least he'd helped me escape the Caldwells out the back door before anyone woke up, presumably all nursing hangovers from the previous night's festivities.

When Trevor had knocked on the bedroom door, I'd thought it was Grant.

Then was hurt and angry when it wasn't.

I'd left the engagement ring on the nightstand, unsure what the hell had actually happened between us.

"Javier!" Felicia yelled.

My other roommate's face appeared in the doorway. "Oh, shit," was his reaction.

"How could you let this happen?" Felicia asked him. "I've been out all day at the flea market for work and I come home to this. You should be checking on her."

"Why would I do that?" he asked, looking annoyed at being called out. "She's an adult. How the hell was I supposed to know what she was doing in here?"

I took another sip of wine, uninterested in their blame-game. "I'm fine. I'm drunk. I'm miserable. I'm wearing a ten-thousand-dollar dress in bed but it's all good. It's a reminder of how stupid I was to think that someone like Grant and someone like me could be together. Forever." I thought about being married to Grant and I wanted to raise my fists in the air and demand answers from a cruel universe.

Not to be dramatic or anything.

Why had I said no? I mean, after I fake said no, and then he told me it was real.

But everything had happened so fast and had all been so confusing and I'd been terrified that I would get in too deep.

Real didn't feel real and getting engaged was crazy impulsive and he'd purposely not told me about the theater and I'd avoided telling him about being fired. And why would I think that he was serious? Who got engaged after two weeks?

The weekend had imploded but now I wanted to talk and the only communication from him was a check that arrived by courier on Monday. There was no note.

"I think I should leave," Javier said. "That's a vibrator lying on the bed next to her and this is very awkward for me."

I glanced over at the pink present from Grant. The vibrator wasn't technically from him which made it even more pathetic that I was treating it like a comfort animal. "I'm not using it. It just reminds me of him."

There was a pause, then Javier said, "See, that doesn't make this any less awkward. Maybe even more."

"I'm sorry I make you uncomfortable," I said, slurring the middle syllable of uncomfortable. "My life is uncomfortable. I am in love with a billionaire and I got fired from the diner. I fucking got fired from the only job between me and starvation and death and it's your fault, Javi."

Felicia gasped. "You got fired?"

I nodded and took another sip. Wine dribbled onto my chin.

Javier's eyebrows rose. "How is this my fault?"

"You didn't warn me hard enough. You told me to go to the Hamptons. Have fun, you said. You didn't tell me not to fall in love with him."

"I thought that was understood. I told you he's a player."

That hurt my heart. Two fat tears squeezed up out of my eyes and rolled down the sides of my cheeks. I picked up the vibrator, needing to emphasis what I was about to say. I pointed it at my roommates. "He is not a player. Don't say that. He's a good man even if he's a control freak and bossy as hell." I sighed, turning my head to see all the designer clothes strewn about my tiny room. "I'm going to die here, aren't I?" I said, pessimism crushing me.

I imagined suffocating under the weight of my dreams and Chanel.

My audition for the role of Cher was in two days and I wasn't prepared.

Spiraling? I was going over Niagara Falls without a barrel.

"Okay, intervention time," Felicia said, approaching my bed. "This has gone too far."

"It has, hasn't it?" I asked her. "It's all gone too far. I should have stayed in my lane, remembered who I was."

"I swear to God, I'm going to slap you," Felicia said, reaching for my bottle. "You've lost your mind. Stay in what lane? Fuck that. Starving actress isn't your identity, it's just your current circumstance. And don't tell me you of all people believe that bullshit that you don't deserve to be in their world of privilege. Who are they? People with money. That's it. They're no better than any of us."

"I don't mean they're better than me. Just that I don't belong there. Taking handouts from rich people. I need to succeed on my own, right?" I didn't resist this time when she reached for the wine. "But I am in love with Grant and now I'm never going to have him. This sucks. Everything sucks."

"Get rid of this," Felicia said, shoving the bottle at Javier.

"Gladly," he said. He went down the hall just as the buzzer

rang.

"Come on," Felicia said. "Sit up." She took my hand and gave it a gentle squeeze. "It's going to be okay, eventually. Maybe you can talk to Grant."

Javier could be heard talking to someone and he reappeared in my doorway. "You got a package."

My heart soared. A gift from Grant? An indicator he wanted to talk to me, to work things out?

My roommate handed me a flat envelope. I frowned and opened it. Two one-hundred-dollar bills fell out. "What the hell is this?"

I shook the envelope. There was no note. I put a bill in each of my hands and held them out to my roommates. "Here. One for each of you."

Javier reached out to take it but Felicia slapped his hand. "Stop it. She's loaded and has no clue what she's doing."

My phone buzzed. Felicia picked it up off my dresser. "You have a text from your boss. He says you can come back to work tomorrow."

"Really?" I grabbed the phone from her. She was right. I could go back to work. "Thank God." I didn't even care to question it. I was just grateful and I shot off a response that may or may not have had a dozen exclamation points and heart eye emojis.

"Why don't you get up and take a shower?" Felicia asked.

I thought about it.

I was an optimist. "I can do that."

Felicia was scooping up piles of designer clothes crumpled on my floor. "I'm steaming these and hanging them up. This is a crime against fashion."

"Thanks, Felicia." My head was spinning. I reached for a water bottle and took a big swig. "You're awesome and I love you." I would have said it sober but drunk it sounded even more effusive. "You're my best friend."

"I love you too." Felicia stood there with a pile of laundry loaded to her chin. "And maybe you don't want to hear this but you can either ignore all the opportunities that came from meeting Grant or you can appreciate them. Yes, you have a broken heart and I'm not discounting that, but you have an audition you never could have gotten on your own. Maybe that's why the universe led him to you. That's what you can learn and take away from this."

"You're right. I don't want to hear that," I said, even as I thought there might be some truth to it. "But you have a point. I need to appreciate this audition and I need to be prepared for it, not nursing a hangover."

"Good girl." She nodded approvingly.

I left my room, holding on to the wall of the narrow hallway for support. Javier was getting an iced coffee out of the fridge. He gave me a cautious glance. "Do you need help?"

"I've got it." I climbed the single step into our bathroom. It felt like Mount Everest. My hand was shaking. "I think I wrecked myself."

"That you did." Javier poured a glass of water. "Here. Drink this. And for the record, don't listen to Felicia. The universe wasn't trying to teach you anything. You met a guy and you fell in love with him. That's not meant to be a lesson. It's meant to be a relationship. If I were you, I'd just go and talk to him. If you care about someone, you don't give up until you've exhausted all possibilities that the relationship will work."

His voice hit me full force. My face got hot and I stared at him, heart racing.

He was one hundred percent right.

"Javi, you're the wisest man in the world."

"Fuck yeah, I am."

After I detoxed from pickling myself with wine and working my "please forgive me" shift at work tomorrow, I was going to Grant's office and we were going to talk. I did know Grant, and he wasn't a man who confessed feelings if he didn't have them.

Everything had gotten out of hand, but that didn't mean we didn't have a future.

No acting. Just straight talk.

CHAPTER 16

Feeling almost human, I went into work at the diner the next morning. I wasn't sleeping well and I couldn't get images out of my head of laughing with Grant, being in bed with Grant, hearing him saying he loved me. It was killing me.

I was shocked Lou had given me my job back so quickly. He must not have been able to find a replacement on such short notice or maybe he'd decided to just give me a written warning. Whatever his reason, I was grateful.

The diner was crowded as usual when I walked in, but I frowned, immediately puzzled. Who the hell was singing? Because he sucked. It wasn't any of my usual co-workers. It was a singing voice I'd never heard and never wanted to again. I looked around, trying to find the source of the off-key baritone. My gaze landed on a guy with broad shoulders wearing the diner uniform of a black T-shirt and jeans, sleeves rolled like greasers in the fifties.

Then he turned and I almost fainted for real this time. It was Grant, attempting Grease Lightning, very unsuccessfully. He gave me a wink.

Theresa appeared at my elbow. "What is happening?" I asked her, heart racing. I was ridiculously, embarrassingly happy to see him.

It had to mean he wanted to talk.

"He sucks, doesn't he?" she asked cheerfully.

"I don't understand." I had no clue whatsoever what was going on.

Lou appeared next to Grant. He made a throat-cutting gesture. Grant stopped singing. Then Lou yelled to me, "Leah! Get up here. Duet."

This was a total setup. I wasn't even sure I had my job back but it was clear Grant had paid Lou to do this. The man loved a grand gesture. This time I decided to roll with it. Why was I even fighting it? Hadn't I always said I loved an entrance?

All eyes were on me. I went over to the counter by the kitchen door where Grant was standing. "What are we singing?" I asked him, trying to act cool.

For a minute he didn't speak. He just stared into my eyes and I saw everything I wanted to see there. Regret. Love. Hope.

Then he started singing, his voice rough. Of course it was Summer Lovin.' I gave him a look, but I joined in right at my part. The strength of my voice seemed to bolster his, and conscious of the fact that he was humiliating himself on my behalf, I entered and exited sooner than necessary, embellishing and playing up the fun aspect of the song. I mostly looked at him, admiring how hot he was in that black T-shirt, but I also engaged with the diners out of habit. When the last note rang out, there was a respectable amount of applause.

Lou, who wasn't known for interacting with the customers, spoke up. "Thanks for being patient with us this morning, folks. If you noticed Grant here does not have a pro voice but he wanted to serenade his girl, and I couldn't resist." He put his hand to his chest. "I've been married to my sweetheart for twenty-five years and I'm a sucker for romance."

He was? That was adorable. Lou talked about his wife on a regular basis but he always acted gruff. Right now, he genuinely looked like he'd wanted to be a part of a moment.

"Back to your regular program," he said now with a grin. "Theresa, sing something."

Theresa stepped forward and launched into "Memories" from Cats.

"What is going on?" I asked Grant, wanting to jump into his arms and kiss his handsome face, but knowing we needed to talk first.

He pulled me into the kitchen. "I'm sorry," he said. "For leaving you in the Hamptons. For being an idiot. For not telling you about the theater. For proposing to you in front of everyone. I'm sorry."

"You should be." Grant cleared his throat. "I am."

"I'm sorry too," I murmured. "I didn't know what to say and everything I said sounded wrong." It hadn't told him anything about the truth of what I felt for him.

He nodded. "I'm here to tell you that I am sorry but also that I have no intention of tearing the theater down. That I know you want to be independent and in control of your own life and choices and I totally respect that. That I'm asking you to be with me, because I love you and you make me happy in a way I could never have imagined."

He reached for me and I didn't resist. Couldn't resist. Why the hell would I resist? "Grant, I love you too. I meant that when I said that. I just didn't think that…" I didn't know how to articulate myself. God, for being an actress I couldn't express myself when it counted.

"Leah," he said, cupping my cheeks and staring at me intently. "I'm a man who has always been alone and I thought I always would be alone. I accepted that because I don't like opening myself up and being in a position to get my heart fucking stomped on. But I never stood a chance with you. You're my person. Do you get that?"

Oh yeah, that was me melting. Straight up puddle. "You're my person too. You're my Grant." The kitchen was loud and hot and staff was moving all around us, but I didn't notice. I'd been in New York too long to be distracted by people. Every day was surrounded by the chaos of the city.

He hauled me against him.

I had a question first before I kissed the stuffing out of him. "Did you pay Lou to get my job back?" I asked.

Grant shook his head. "No. I struck a deal with Lou. I worked a shift here yesterday in exchange for you getting your job back. He was short-staffed and I think he wanted to see the rich guy waiting tables and washing dishes. Little did he know, I washed dishes in the navy."

That made me grin despite my confusion and mixed feelings. "You definitely ruined it for him. He likes to torture people."

"Did you get the tips I had delivered to you last night?"

For a second I didn't know what he was talking about. Then I remembered the two hundred bucks that had showed up on our doorstep when I'd been a bottle and a half into a chardonnay pity party. "I did, thanks. I'm impressed with your haul." I usually made more than that, but for a novice, he hadn't done bad.

"Thank you." He caressed my bottom lip with his thumb and gave me a look that made me weak in the knees.

"What is it you want exactly, Grant?" I asked softly. "For real."

"For real I want whatever you want as long as you'll let me in your life. I just want to be with you in whatever way works for you."

I closed my eyes briefly, knowing I was way too in love with him to say anything other than yes. "Do you really think two people who barely know each other can make a serious relationship work? Could make marriage work?"

"Who says we barely know each other? You know me, Leah, despite what I said at my parents' house. And I know you."

He was right. "I do love you, Grant. It may be crazy, but I do know you, and you're a good man. My man." Javier was right. We could either make it work or not. It was up to us and I couldn't let fear of failure stop me. Because that's all it was. Fear.

"Does that mean you see us dating? Because I have to tell you,

I will serenade you every day until you give me another chance."

That made me laugh. "That's so not necessary. But yes. Dating. Living together. Getting married. Driving your family nuts together. The whole happily ever after."

"Then I guess there's only one thing left to do."

"What's that?"

"I'm going to kiss you."

And he did. He kissed me like there was no tomorrow. Like I was the only woman in the world. Like he was out of air and I was oxygen.

I threw my arms around his neck and kissed him back, loving the way he tasted, felt, sounded. Loving him.

One of the cooks catcalled and we broke apart, breathing hard.

"Hi, Grant," I murmured, gazing up at him with a soft smile.

"Hi, Leah."

The kitchen door swung open. "Leah! Get out here. Fun's over. Hit the bricks, Caldwell."

"I have to go," I said, amused.

"Apparently, I do too. I'll see you after work. I'll be right here when you get off."

Nothing sounded better than that. "I feel like there is a double meaning in that." "There is. And I feel like you don't like my singing."

I gave him a smirk, deliriously happy. "Stick to real estate, Caldwell."

I produced the plate of chocolate chip pancakes and set it in front of Leah with a flourish. "Merry Christmas, baby."

"Wow, I'm impressed." Leah gave me a sleepy, sexy smile and yawned. "Thank you, sweetheart. Rose would be proud of you."

"Trust me, I'm sending her a picture of my work. Here's your coffee." I had gotten up early to surprise her with my culinary skills. I'd been practicing the pancakes for a few weeks. Turned out it wasn't that hard, but the flip was a certain skill set I hadn't previously possessed. I was in my underwear and she was in my T-shirt, sporting some serious "just fucked" hair. Which she had been. Repeatedly.

"Mm, I need that. You kept me up late."

I had. My cock hardened at the memory. "We're in Fiji on a private island and I owed you a hundred orgasms. I had to make some serious headway."

She sighed with contentment. "You definitely did." She sipped her coffee again and put her fork through the pancakes. "I love you."

"I love you, too." The last two months with Leah had been the best of my entire life. She made me feel light, happy, content. She made me laugh. "I'm proud of you, by the way. My little Nikki Sixx."

She hadn't gotten the part of young Cher that Gigi had arranged the audition for, but the very next week she'd gotten a chorus girl role entirely on her own. It was for a long-running show and she'd made the decision to give up the server position at the diner. It was a huge step for her, and I was thrilled she was finding her success. Though I was going to miss that poodle skirt. Fond memories of tugging that fabric up came to mind.

Leah laughed. "You know what? I'm proud of me too."

"Good." I poured myself a cup of coffee and leaned over the counter in front of her, watching my beautiful soulmate eat, the backdrop of crystalline blue water behind her. Yes, I said it. Soulmate. Leah was it for me. "Are you ready to get married today?"

"One hundred percent."

Leah had agreed to marry me, which amazed me, but I wasn't going to question it. We had just moved into an apartment together, and because she was independent and proud, we were splitting the rent. I think when I actually agreed to that without question, knowing I'd be living in a shoebox with a crap bathroom, she had realized how fucking serious I was about this relationship. I'd had to jettison ninety percent of my belongings. She had taken to calling me the "billionaire in a box." She could call me whatever she wanted as long as I could call her mine. Besides, I liked being on top of her. And I meant that exactly how you think.

"I've never been more prepared for any role than that of your wife."

I growled and reached for her. She laughed and tried to get up and escape, but I caught her and hauled her back to the bedroom.

"Who's faking it now?" I asked her twenty minutes later as she shattered beneath me.

"Not your fiancé," she murmured, eyes glazed with love and pleasure.

Within two hours, we said "I do" on a yacht on the water with no one but the officiant.

No circus.

Just me and her.

Then we jumped overboard.

.

CPSIA information can be obtained
at www.ICGtesting.com
Printed in the USA
BVHW032011090220
571849BV00017B/88